SHORT CUTS

INTRODUCTIONS TO FILM STUDIES

MUSIC IN FILM

SOUNDTRACKS AND SYNERGY

PAULINE REAY

WALLFLOWER

LONDON and NEW YORK

A Wallflower Paperback

First published in Great Britain in 2004 by
Wallflower Press
4th Floor, 26 Shacklewell Lane, London E8 2EZ
www.wallflowerpress.co.uk

A catalogue record for this book is available from the British Library

ISBN 1 903364 65 5

Book Design by Rob Bowden Design

Printed in Great Britain by Antony Rowe Ltd, Chippenham, Wiltshire

CONTENTS

ACKNOWLEDGEMENTS

I would like to thank those people who have supported me throughout the writing of this book. In particular I would like to thank Sam Lay; this book would not have been written without her help and encouragement. I would also like to thank Symon Quy and Ian Bell for their comments on the drafts and many useful discussions.

Thanks also to Yoram Allon and Hannah Patterson at Wallflower Press for their patience and support throughout the writing of this book, to David Butler for his constructive comments on an early draft, and to staff at the BFI for help with sourcing illustrations.

Finally, love and thanks to Tim and Hal for giving me the time and space to do this – I couldn't have done it without you!

INTRODUCTION

Despite the popularity of film and the fact that a large amount of film music is heard by a mass audience, academic writing in the field of film music has been somewhat neglected over the years. The main reason for this is that film music brings together two discrete areas each with their own specialist language and terminology. Those who have written on film music tend to be either from a film studies background with no specialist knowledge of music studies or from a musicology background with no specialist understanding of film studies. Once this is taken into consideration, it is not difficult to see why academic writing in this area has been somewhat limited.

Whilst there have been relatively few academic studies of film music there are a large number of publications available which cater for the fan market and soundtrack collectors ranging from biographical studies of particular composers, to journals such as *Soundtrack!* and numerous websites.[1] This problem with academic writing about film music has itself been discussed in recent work on the area.[2] K. J. Donnelly comments,

> Whilst film scholarship has largely ignored film music as a problem it would rather not face, music scholarship has persisted in the prejudice that film music is somehow below the standard of absolute music. (2001a: 1)

Whilst David Neumeyer, Caryl Flinn and James Buhler note,

> Film music's interdisciplinarity, like that of the cinema itself, produces and is produced by a wide array of methodologies that can sometimes operate in direct conflict with one another. (2000: 3)

The main intentions of this book are firstly, to give a critical overview of film music in American and European films whilst placing it within historical and cultural contexts; and secondly, to focus on the use of popular idioms in film music and explore areas that have been largely neglected in other publications. There are three main themes running throughout the book: firstly, the prevalence of popular music in film and its perceived inferiority; secondly, the perceived superiority of the original score and the assumption that films need original music; and thirdly, the use of music as a marketing tool. All three are closely connected and have been a part of film music from the beginning of cinema.

Throughout the book reference will be made to the approaches and theories that have been applied to film music, in particular, the work of Claudia Gorbman and Jeff Smith. Gorbman's book *Unheard Melodies* (1987) explores the notion that film music is unheard and focuses on examples from *classical Hollywood film scores** to discuss how music is used in film. Smith's book *The Sounds of Commerce* (1998) explores the use of pop music in film and considers both the textual and commercial uses of music in film. It is necessary here to clarify the terms 'textual' and 'extra-textual', which are used here to discuss film music. Textual is used to discuss how music operates as a part of the film text, whilst extra-textual is used to discuss the areas of industry organisation, technology, critical attitudes and *synergy** which are outside of the film text; in addition the term 'commercial' is used to discuss how music is used as a marketing tool in film.

Chapter one gives a historical overview of film music as it has evolved from the early days of silent cinema, through the classical Hollywood and post-classical eras to the present day. This chapter considers industry organisation, technology, critical attitudes and textual conventions introducing the terms *diegetic** and *nondiegetic**, which have been used for the placing of music in film. Whilst each period has seen many changes, it is in the post-classical era where these have been the most pronounced. These changes include popular genres of music being used nondiegetically, the growing popularity of scores compiled from prerecorded songs and the increased importance of the music supervisor. Whilst popular music has been a part of film since the beginning of cinema, its increasing use, and its effect on the market for film music, has been responsible for influencing the direction of film music in this post-classical era.

----

* terms indicated with an asterisk throughout the book are defined in the glossary

Chapter two provides the basic tools for understanding the textual functions of film music, which will be put to use in the later chapters. The chapter briefly outlines the place of music in the film soundtrack and then goes on to explore some of the theories about the textual functions of film music in the classical Hollywood score and in scores compiled from pop music. These theories are then applied to contemporary examples, which consider how music operates as an integral part of the *mise-en-scène*, its narrative function and its cultural connotations. Danny Elfman's original classical score for Tim Burton's *Edward Scissorhands* (1990) is discussed. This is followed by two case studies: the first explores the use of music in the European art film and the work of Rainer Werner Fassbinder and Pedro Almodóvar; and the second explores the use of popular music in the score for Martin Scorsese's *GoodFellas* (1990). The next two chapters are mainly concerned with contemporary film music and pursue areas that are relatively unexplored. *Magnolia* (1999), directed by Paul Thomas Anderson, used the songs of singer-songwriter Aimee Mann as inspiration for the script. Anderson intended to adapt Mann's music for the screen in the same way a book would be adapted. Whilst there are numerous examples of films named after pop songs,[3] there are still relatively few examples of pop songs actually influencing the writing of film scripts. This is the focus of chapter three which includes a case study of Magnolia as well as discussion of the way in which popular songs have influenced films such as *The Graduate* (Mike Nichols, 1967), *McCabe and Mrs Miller* (Robert Altman, 1971) and *Singles* (Cameron Crowe, 1992). This demonstrates how popular music can be used as an integral part of the film narrative and is evidence of the increasing influence of popular music on film.

Since the 1960s pop and rock musicians have become increasingly involved in the writing of film scores. Chapter four chronicles the involvement of popular musicians in film music and examines the reasons for this discussing examples including *The Virgin Suicides* (Sofia Coppola, 1999) composed by French electronic duo, Air; the film scores of ex-Velvet Underground member John Cale; the collaborations between British independent band Tindersticks and French director Claire Denis and the work of ex-Devo member Mark Mothersbaugh. The chapter closes with a case study of Damon Albarn, a member of the band Blur who has recently composed three film scores, including a collaboration with Michael Nyman.

Chapter five explores the use of music as a marketing tool in film. Whilst synergy and the cross-promotion between the film and music industries is generally thought of as being a relatively new phenomenon this chapter demonstrates that this cross-promotion has in fact been present since the early days of silent cinema. Beginning with examples from the silent to sound and then the classical Hollywood eras, there is then discussion of the commercial implications of the increasing use of pop music in film, considering Henry Mancini's work in the 1960s and the rise of the pop soundtrack in the 1970s. The development of such synergy and the emergence of new media forms in the 1980s are then discussed in some detail. Consideration is also given to the rise of the soundtrack as a cultural product and the diversification of the genre and fragmentation of the market in the 1990s. Some of the more recent well-known examples of synergy in films such as *Reservoir Dogs* (Quentin Tarantino, 1992), *Pulp Fiction* (Quentin Tarantino, 1994) and *Trainspotting* (Danny Boyle, 1996) are discussed. The chapter also considers the economic and aesthetic implications of dealing with film soundtracks for directors working outside of the mainstream, using examples from the films of Wim Wenders and Jim Jarmusch.

The conclusion summarises the main debates and discusses the challenges facing film music at the beginning of this millennium and considers the future for the film soundtrack in the new digital multimedia age.

Film music is a huge area and this introduction cannot consider the area in the detail that is clearly necessary. However, what I have attempted to do is give an overview of film music to date and then discuss some of the neglected areas in more detail. There are many other areas of interest which are not discussed here or elsewhere: collaborations between particular directors and composers; directors who compose music for their own films; directors such as Derek Jarman and those of the French New Wave who see the score as having a life of its own; artists such as Barry Adamson who have composed music for non-existent films and the approach to music of the Dogme 95 filmmakers.[4] It is also important to state here that this book is not attempting to cover the musical genre, the pop/rock biopic, rock documentaries, or any biographical studies of particular composers.

The book is written from a film studies perspective, and takes into account my own personal interest in film music. I do not use any specialist terms associated with the study of music and the intention is for what follows to be accessible to students on film and media studies courses, those studying film music, as well as individuals with a general interest in film music. I hope that this opens up the area of discussion on film music to a wider audience and encourages readers to pursue their interests further.

1   FILM MUSIC: A HISTORICAL OVERVIEW

This opening chapter aims to give a historical overview of film music as it has evolved from the early days of silent cinema to the present day. As this is a huge area it will only be possible to outline key events and use brief examples of film scores; however, reference will be given to other works in this area. For clarity this chapter will be divided into three sections to discuss firstly, the silent to early sound era; secondly, the *classical Hollywood** era; and thirdly, the post-classical era. Within each section consideration will be given to extra-textual elements, examining the impact industry organisation and technology have had on film music, as well as critical attitudes to film music and the textual conventions of film music in each period.

From the silent era to early sound films (1895–1930)

> For the first thirty years of the cinema's existence the films may
> have been silent but the places in which they were shown rarely
> were. (French 2001)

The so-called 'silent cinema' was never actually silent, from as early as the beginning of the nineteenth century sound effects were used to accompany projected images and on 28 December 1895 a Lumière programme in Paris had piano accompaniment. Musical accompaniment was important not only for audiences but also in the production process, with musicians employed in the studio to help create moods for actors, and also to counteract the noise in studios where two films would often be being made on the same stage. There are many explanations proposed to account for music's presence from the early days of cinema. Music had the practical task of drowning out or covering up the noise of the projector (Gorbman 1987: 36; Brown 1994: 12); as well as being needed, psychologically, to smooth over natural human fears of darkness and silence (Brown 1994: 12).

Both the function and conventions of early cinema music were influenced by traditions established in nineteenth-century theatrical melodrama; forms such as the music hall, theatre and opera all exerted an influence on film music. The actual physical context of the cinema at this time and the fact that films were often shown in a theatrical setting was of great importance. Martin Marks (1996a) discusses the variations in accompaniment to silent film, determined largely by the time period and theatrical milieu, using four distinct categories. The first of these being between the mid-1890s and early 1900s when vaudeville/music hall orchestras accompanied films seen as part of variety shows. The second period, from 1905, marks the nickelodeon boom, which led to mass audiences for films. As films moved into theatres of their own, music came with them, principally on pianos or mechanical equivalents; this also marks the beginning of film music as a distinct profession, although many pianos were out of tune and many performers unskilled. During the third period, from about 1910, theatres tended to be larger with more impressive facilities and increased budgets for music. This coincided with radical changes in film production and distribution and led to a growing market for musical arrangements suitable for film-playing. There was also an increasing number of theatres with more than one projector so film lengths could increase, leading to the 'epic' format used by directors such as D. W. Griffith. The late 1910s and 1920s saw the final period, that of the grand movie 'palaces' with spectacular theatre organs sharing the spotlight with large orchestras and colourful conductors. During this period shows became lavish, mixing concert overtures, vaudeville stars, classical performers and skits intended as prologues to actual films.

This period also saw the beginning of the movement towards *vertical integration**. Growing *convergence** reduced the independence of exhibitors, as the power to control the music to accompany films passed from the exhibitors to the production companies. Throughout this period Hollywood invested in songwriters, composers and music publishing houses; with Paramount and Loew's being the first to buy their own publishing houses followed by the Warner Bros. purchase of the original Tin Pan Alley house, M. Witmark & Sons in 1929. Film companies were now in a position to generate added revenues from the songs featured in films. *Photoplay* commented in 1929,

> It is now a question as to which has absorbed which. Is the motion picture industry a subsidiary of the music publishing business – or have film producers gone into the business of marketing songs? (cited in Mundy 1999: 51)

Closely connected with these changes in industry organisation are the developments in technology made during this period, particularly the move to the full commercial introduction of synchronised sound in the cinema in the mid-to-late 1920s. A crucial difference between live music for silent films and music in the sound film is that whilst the former is live and continuous, the latter is recorded and the recording required the use of new technology. Throughout the silent period various gramophone synchronisers were developed for use with films. In 1895 Thomas Edison introduced the kinetophone, which combined the moving images of his kinetoscope with the phonograph; however, the cost was high and demand for synchronised films remained low. In 1903 one of Edison's commercial rivals, Sigmund Lubin, marketed a series of 'song films', and in 1904 Lubin marketed his cinephone, offering a 'Combination of Instrumental Music, Song and Speech with Life Motion Pictures'. Lubin's cinephone provided only primitive synchronisation and proved a commercial failure. The first system in Britain was the Chronophone in 1904 and in 1907 Cecil Hepworth's company launched the Vivaphone, a synchronised disc system which was successful for many years in producing short films of music-hall turns, limited in length by the playing-time of the gramophone disc. However, as Roger Manvell and John Huntley note, 'The quality of the sound remained poor, and the advancing technique of the film soon made it desirable for full-length productions to be accompanied by piano and orchestra' (1975: 17).

During the First World War new developments were kept on hold and were not seriously reintroduced until 1923, with the introduction of the Phonofilm system which, rather than being disc-based, was sound-on-film (optical sound recording). By 1924 more than thirty theatres in the US were wired up for Phonofilm, and in 1925 Fox bought the patents from the inventor Lee deForest. A year later they also bought the US patents of the German Tri-Ergon system, and the merged technology became known as Movietone from 1927. In the meantime, in 1925 Vitaphone, Warner Bros. and Western Electric had begun to develop sound-on-disc film projects, particularly music-based. When Fox's Movietone sound shorts premiered in 1927, they were competition for Warner Bros.' Vitaphone programmes. The move from sound-on-disc to sound-on-film was of great importance in the development of the sound film as it facilitated the synchronising of dialogue. However, this also brought with it new restrictions; as synchronised sound meant actors were obliged to remain close to the microphones. The perils of sound at this time are comically illustrated in the 1952 musical *Singin' in the Rain* (Gene Kelly/Stanley Donen).

Warner Bros.' Vitaphone programmes premiered in August 1926 and reflected their interest in using the system to provide recorded musical accompaniment rather than making 'talkie' features. The first show was hugely successful and ran for eight months with the ability to offer exhibitors pre-recorded music to replace increasingly costly live music a major attraction. By October 1926, when the second Vitaphone programme premiered, the short musical items which accompanied the feature film, *The Better 'Ole*, were much more popular.[1] As Vitaphone programmes increased in length and number audiences became disenchanted; this along with competition from Fox's Movietone shorts encouraged Warner Bros. to make the decision to invest in a synchronised-sound feature film.

Whilst *The Jazz Singer* (Alan Crosland, 1927) is widely known as the first feature-length sound film, the earliest example is another Warner Bros. production, *Don Juan* (directed by Alan Crosland), which premiered in August 1926. *Don Juan* was not a talking picture but featured a musical score recorded on discs using the Vitaphone system of sound synchronisation to accompany the images, the score was a compilation mixed with some original music. Warner Bros. followed this the next year with *The Jazz Singer*, which also used the Vitaphone process and concentrated on the synchronised performances of songs and dialogue.

By 1909 much of the writing about film music was in trade paper editorials, letters and articles calling for the improvement of music. That same year an editorial in *The Moving Picture World* complained that in too many outlets pianos were old and out of tune; also that the music often had little relation to events on screen, and sometimes finished before the end of the film! By 1910 *The Moving Picture World* and *Moving Picture News* began to carry regular columns to discuss film music, the former having an advice column on 'Music for the Picture' (Marks 1997: 10; Lack 1997: 46).

In 1927 composers Hans Erdmann and Giuseppe Becce approached the question 'Do films really *need* music?' in their text on music in the silent film. They pointed out that music is not generally considered a part of the production process of a film but belongs to theatre performance and that, 'film practice has acted as if – indeed, has decided that – films cannot be without music' (quoted in Buhler *et al.* 2000: 9–10). The question 'Do films really *need* music?' would be frequently asked as film music continued to develop.

Composer and writer Irwin Bazelon identifies four types of music being used during the silent period: (i) piano improvisation; (ii) published musical extracts (*cue** sheets); (iii) the score, being principally derived from familiar musical sources; and (iv) original scores, created for specific films, sometimes by eminent composers (1975: 18–19). This music was comprised of both *classical* and popular pieces; popular music having been part of film from this period. Rick Altman notes how

> Film music scholarship has concentrated almost exclusively on 'classical' music. Yet the influence of the nickelodeon's song-oriented accompaniment practices is visible throughout the history of film music. (2001: 26)[2]

From around 1909 distributors sent out cue music sheets to cinemas, these comprised of 'brief lists of specific pieces and/or types of music to accompany particular films, with cues and supplementary instructions' (Marks 1996a: 86). The emergence of the cue sheet was a sign that film music needed to be dramatically motivated, a direct influence from the theatrical tradition. The concept of originality is of interest here; Claudia Gorbman quotes Max Winkler, one of several who each take credit for having invented the cue sheet around 1911, reminiscing,

> We turned to crime. We began to dismember the great masters. We murdered the works of Beethoven, Mozart, Grieg, J. S. Bach, Verdi, Bizet, Tchaikovsky and Wagner – everything that wasn't protected by copyright from our pilfering. (1987: 167[n])

Marks notes that complete original scores were simply not feasible:

> Most films were too short-lived, the distribution system too far-
> flung, and performers too varied in ensemble and too uneven in
> talent to justify commissioned scores. (Marks 1996a: 186)

Kathryn Kalinak also notes how the basis of the conventional practice
established in the early collections of cue sheets was that the works of
composers such as those mentioned by Winkler constituted the backbone
of musical encyclopedias and libraries. However, despite this she notes
a common complaint was from the unsympathetic theatre owner who
insisted on popular music (1992: 61) – an interesting precursor of the
practice that became prevalent in the 1980s and 1990s with both film
production companies and record companies keen to use popular music
in their films.

In 1913 J. S. Zamecnik's work of classified mood music for silent pia-
nists, 'The Sam Fox Moving Picture Music Volumes', was an attempt to
provide suitable mood music for most common film themes, for example,
'Indian Attack' and 'Fairy Music'. Whilst at first, cue sheets were rather
unsophisticated and sometimes unreliable, over time they became more
sophisticated and commercially valuable. Erno Rapée's *Motion Picture
Moods* (1924) was the most impressive single book of piano music. Rapée
followed this in 1925 with *Encyclopedia of Music for Pictures*, offering more
than 5,000 titles of published arrangements under 500 headings. Russell
Lack notes how, despite Rapée's relatively high profile as a composer, he
felt that if the audience came out of the theatre almost unaware of the
musical accompaniment to the film, the work of the musical director has
been successful (1997: 34); an early indication of the notion of the 'inaudibility' of film music.

Scores derived from familiar musical sources, or compiled scores,
became a great tradition of film music with Joseph Breil's landmark score
for *Birth of a Nation* (D. W. Griffith, 1915). The score includes original music,
folk melodies, well-known classical sections – including Wagner's 'Ride
of the Valkyries' – and well-known traditional pieces such as 'The Star-
Spangled Banner' and 'Dixie'. Due to the range of music included critics
have described the score as a 'pastiche' (Prendergast 1992: 13, Manvell
and Huntley 1975: 26). However, as Lack points out, this represents,
'one of the first deliberate attempts to create a score specifically for a
single picture' (1997: 34). The score was important for its influence on the
development of film orchestration in the US and Europe and for its role

in pioneering the compilation score. Compiled scores were still played by performers in the cinema but were 'liable to be altered from performance to performance' (Marks 1996: 187). This was often dependent on the cinema; larger cinemas tended to have a full orchestra whereas small cinemas would only have a piano and there were many variations in between.

As well as the many compiled scores, original scores were still being written. In 1908 Camille Saint-Saëns' score for *L'Assassinat du Duc de Guise* (André Calmettes/Charles Le Bargy) was one of the first high-profile original film scores written by an established classical composer. Original film scores increased in number in the 1920s and whilst there tends to be an emphasis on the dominance of the US in the development of film sound and music, with regards to original scores some of the most impressive work originated from outside of the US, in France, Germany and Russia. These include Erik Satie's score for *Entr'acte* (René Clair, 1924), Edmund Meisel's scores for *Battleship Potemkin* (Sergei Eisenstein, 1925) and *October* (Sergei Eisenstein, 1927), Arthur Honegger's scores for *La Roue* (Abel Gance, 1924) and *Napoléon* (Abel Gance, 1927), and Dmitri Shostakovich's score for *The New Babylon* (Grigori Kozintsev/Leonid Trauberg, 1929). Meisel's score for Eisenstein's *Battleship Potemkin* represented a key advance in film technique, being a sound film 'where music supplied more than simply an illustration of screen content' (Lack 1997: 39). Meisel worked closely with Eisenstein on the score, trying to prove 'that there was a formal correlation between the montage of a film and music' (Prendergast 1992: 15).[3]

A number of writers have commented on the use of compiled and original scores in silent film. John Mundy notes:

> It is clear that the emerging technique of film scoring for 'silent' films relied upon mixing original composition with compilations from existing, often classical, music. This meant that film scores, though they might include segments from what were then regarded as 'popular' light classics, were not 'popular music' in the sense that we understand it today. (1999: 17)

Whilst these segments may not be 'popular music' in the sense that we understand it today, they were still 'popular' pieces of music, which were significantly different to the more traditional classical music being used. Much of this 'lighter' music was already familiar to the audience; again another similarity with scoring in contemporary films where pop music is often used as a lighter part to the orchestral score.

It is necessary to outline here the terms used for the placing of music in films, diegetic and nondiegetic. The term diegetic relates to the diegesis of the film – the story-world depicted on screen. Here, the 'source' of diegetic music can be observed on screen, for example a character is shown listening to the radio, music being performed live. Nondiegetic music is music that appears to come from outside the story-world, it is often heard as background music and is usually added to the film in postproduction. These terms have been used since Claudia Gorbman's book *Unheard Melodies* drew on narrative theory and applied the terms diegetic and nondiegetic to music. Prior to this the terms 'source' and 'background' music were used, diegetic being previously referred to as source music and nondiegetic being previously referred to as background scoring.[4]

Up until the introduction of sound film, music was predominantly nondiegetic, emanating from the world outside of the film. This changed with the introduction of sound film as in order to give a sense of realism music needed to be seen as diegetic and coming from a visible source. Film music did not respond to the introduction of sound technology with a definitive model for its use; there were many variations with some films using music as it had been used in the silent film, others using music only diegetically, whilst others used continuous nondiegetic accompaniment in some scenes and strict diegetic fidelity in others (Kalinak 1992: 68).

New technologies played a major role in the development of film music during this period with the textual uses of music being largely determined by what the technology allowed. With the introduction of sound into cinema, the film, theatre, radio and music industries began to work together to further the mutual economic interests they shared. This was to have a major impact on cross-promotional practices in an attempt to maximise the profits available from sound film and its symbiotic relationship with music.

The classical Hollywood era (1930–1960)

During this classical era many of the dominant practices of film production were developed as a direct response to the way in which the industry was organised and to the standardisation of technologies. This section covers the period which is often referred to as the 'classical Hollywood' era of the

1930s and 1940s as well as the 'crossover period' into the post-classical era, encompassing the 1950s.

The studio system was the dominant mode of production in Hollywood during this classical period with the film industry being comprised of eight companies known as 'the big five' and 'the little three'. The big five being Paramount, Fox, Metro-Goldwyn-Mayer (MGM), Warner Bros. and RKO; and the little three Universal, United Artists and Columbia. Between 1930 and 1948 the eight majors between them controlled ninety-five per cent of all films exhibited in the USA, and there was a booming and sophisticated, vertically integrated system in place whereby the major studios controlled the modes of production, distribution and exhibition.

The major studios operated efficiently using assembly-line production, which was kept moving with a highly diversified division of labour. This division of labour was in place throughout each of the studios as a whole, including the music department. The music departments were an essential component of the Hollywood studio system and comprised of the studio's music director, composers, orchestrators, recording engineers – with numerous categories of specialists such as main title specialists, 'chase' specialists and so on. The Hollywood production model also dictated the timeframe in which composers were expected to work, and scores were almost always not composed until after the film was shot. The period of time given to the composer varied from as little as three weeks (or less) to six weeks. It was also not uncommon for a composer to work on a number of productions simultaneously, or for several composers to work on one production simultaneously.

During this classical era, the power and creative control was with the producers and the studios; directors, actors and composers were merely contracted to do a specific job; Marks describes composers as 'subordinates under contract to studio music departments' (1996b: 251). Lack notes how the status and authority of composers was further eroded in the 1930s with the creation of long-term contracts between composers, musicians, orchestrators and studios. This tied them together for a number of projects and meant many studios denied composers the right to use their own music in any other context (1997: 126). Despite these restrictions, there were various advantages to working in the studio system for the composer. Marks notes that they had 'financial security, a position in a circle of highly talented musicians, and the knowledge that their music could be heard by millions' (1996b: 251).

In 1948 the majors suffered a reversal in fortune when some exhibitors brought an anti-trust action to put an end to the film industry's monopoly over exhibition. This was the first step in the demise of the studio system and led to the Supreme Court issuing decrees that effectively divested the majors of their power as vertically integrated systems on the grounds of unfair practices.

This led to an increase in *independent** production and a trend towards diversification and conglomeration. Hollywood's involvement with the music industry continued; in 1930 Warner Bros. followed its purchase of several music-publishing houses by buying Brunswick Records. However, this involvement was minimal until MGM started up its own subsidiary in the mid-1940s. This was followed by Decca's purchase of Universal in 1952, which also led the other Hollywood majors to start up or acquire record subsidiaries between 1957 and 1958 and both Decca and Universal were acquired by MCA in 1959. Reasons for this involvement included the overall climate of diversification and conglomeration, the shrinking sheet music market, and the sudden boom in record sales. Alexander Doty describes how these *conglomerates**

> signaled the creation of a network of potential publicity sources for film promoters, as most conglomerate entertainment divisions had recording and television subsidiaries and often acquired interests in other related properties. (1988: 72)

In addition to these changes in industry organisation, the period between the mid-1930s and the mid-1940s saw technological, as well as stylistic standardisation, in film music. Recording technology improved in the 1950s and technological developments such as the increased use of colour photography, the introduction of widescreen processes, and adoption of stereophonic sound and magnetic tracks were all to have an impact on films and film music, as was the challenge of new entertainment technologies such as television.

The move to widescreen presentation throughout the 1950s brought films recorded with magnetic stereo sound, a superior recording method designed to take over from the optical soundtrack. Whilst a number of films were recorded using the magnetic soundtrack during the late 1950s the majority of actual release prints were still printed with optical soundtracks. Theatre owners were reluctant to upgrade their projection equipment to cope with yet another change and this led to a two-tier exhibition circuit – with some theatres showing stereo and others mono versions of the same film, ticket prices naturally reflected the perceived difference in quality (Lack 1997: 156).

By the mid-1930s a number of critical studies of the sound film appeared, some of which gave consideration to film music, coinciding with the emergence of the standardised score. The Academy of Motion Picture Arts and Sciences offered official recognition by adding the originally-composed film score as an award category in 1934. In *Film Music* (1936), Kurt London comments on the lack of seriousness with which film music was treated:

> The music which accompanies the film is still struggling for its place in the sun; the film people themselves invariably treat it very casually and are not quite clear in their own minds about its importance; musicians take it up more for the sake of fees than for art's sake … the public finally does not trouble overmuch about music because it always fails to understand the cause and effect of film musical ideas. (1936: 126)

In the early 1930s composer Virgil Thomson addressed the question of whether films need music; his opinion being that music provides temporal rhythms or continuity that film does not possess on its own (cited in Buhler *et al.* 2000: 10). He also raised the question: 'What roles and types of music worked best in a medium which had once been purely visual but could now be heard as well as seen?' (quoted in Marks 1996b: 248). Thomson went on to compose his own film scores and as late as 1945 argued that the feature film still poses problems for the composition of music, identifying dialogue as the culprit as it interrupts the musical continuity (Buhler *et al.* 2000: 10).

However, probably the most important contribution to discussions of film music in the 1940s, and still influential today, is that by Hans Eisler and Theodore Adorno. In *Composing for the Films* (1948), they examine the standardisation of film music and its effect on audiences. The first chapter, 'Prejudices and Bad Habits', discusses the *leitmotif,** unobtrusiveness, visual justification, illustration, stock music, clichés and standardised interpretations. Eisler and Adorno believe these prejudices have hindered the progress of motion-picture music and 'only seem to make sense as a consequence of standardisation within the industry itself, which calls for standard practices everywhere' (1948: 3). They believe the leitmotif enables the composer to quote where otherwise he would have to invent (1948: 4) and question the idea that film music should be unobtrusive stating this is 'one of the most widespread prejudices in the motion-picture industry' (1948: 9). Criticism is also made of the use of stock music, such as the use of the overture of William Tell for thunderstorms, Mendelssohn's wedding march for weddings and so on (1948: 15) believing that all of these relate to a more general state of affairs:

> Mass production of motion pictures has led to the elaboration of typical situations, ever-recurring emotional crises, and standardised methods of arousing suspense. They correspond to cliché effects in music. (1948: 16)

The use of the leitmotif in Hollywood was also criticised by others in the musical community. Aaron Copland, who had composed scores for some major independent American films including *Of Mice and Men* (Lewis Milestone, 1939), without the use of leitmotifs, cited 'the leitmotif's inappropriateness for the screen as well as decrying its formulaic predictability' (quoted in Kalinak 1992: 104).

The concern with realism during the introduction of sound film meant that in 1931 films used almost no nondiegetic music. Gorbman notes how composer Max Steiner stated that sound producers before 1932 considered background music unacceptable, fearing that spectators would demand to know where the music was coming from (1987: 54). Kalinak discusses how the nondiegetic presence of music threatened the invisibility of film and how composers faced the paradoxical perception that good film music is 'inaudible' (1992: 79). Nevertheless in the following years, nondiegetic music was established as a prime component of the classical cinema.[5]

This era saw the development of what became known as '*the classical Hollywood film score*'. Original scores were written specially for films, a change from the compiled scores with some original music that had prevailed in the silent to sound era. Kalinak suggests that the form of the classical Hollywood film score is based upon,

> a set of conventions for the composition and placement of nondiegetic music, which prioritised narrative exposition. These

conventions included the use of music to sustain structural unity; music to illustrate narrative content ... and the privileging of dialogue over other elements of the soundtrack. The medium of the classical Hollywood film score was largely symphonic; its idiom romantic; and its formal unity typically derived from the principle of the leitmotif. (1992: 79)

This standardised 'classical model' was almost immediately absorbed into Hollywood practice, reflecting and reinforcing the industry organisation of the time. Three composers dominated the classical film score in the 1930s: Max Steiner, Alfred Newman and Erich Wolfgang Korngold. All three set the main idiom of musical accompaniment for film as neo-romantic and established its medium as symphonic. Kalinak discusses how Steiner's score for *Cimarron* (Wesley Ruggles, 1931), distinguished by a selective use of nondiegetic music for dramatic emphasis, laid the groundwork for a definitive practice which would evolve into the classical Hollywood film score; this was solidified with the success of *King Kong* (Merian C. Cooper and Ernest B. Schoedsack, 1933) and others (1992: 71). Steiner's work is often used as one of the main examples of classical Hollywood scoring practice. It is easy to characterise, using a lush symphonic style and with a strong emphasis on coordinating music and narrative, often through the use of *mickey-mousing**. Steiner was on the staff at Warner Bros. from 1936 to 1965 before moving to RKO as musical director.[6] Newman scored his first film *Street Scene* (directed by King Vidor) in 1931 and went on to score a diverse range of films including *The Prisoner of Zenda* (John Cromwell, 1937) and *Wuthering Heights* (William Wyler, 1939). He became musical director at United Artists and then at Twentieth Century Fox, where he composed the music for the Twentieth Century Fox logo still in use today. Korngold's work included huge vibrant cues, rousing marches and passionate, romantic melodies. Kalinak uses Korngold's score for *Captain Blood* (Michael Curtiz, 1935) to demonstrate key techniques and practices that characterise the classical model (1992: 79–110).

During the 1940s both the idiom and the medium of the classical Hollywood score began to diversify due to the influx of new composers to Hollywood. One new composer was Bernard Herrmann, who moved away from a dependence on late romanticism, avoiding emotional underscoring and scoring films sparingly, often avoiding a direct correlation between music and screen action. He also composed very short and often unmelodic cues, some lasting only a few seconds and used smaller ensemble rather than the standard symphonic orchestra. This led to him developing a distinctive 'voice' as is demonstrated in his work on films such as *The Magnificent Ambersons* (Orson Welles, 1942) and *Hangover Square* (John Brahm, 1945) and many of the films he worked on with Alfred Hitchcock, most famously *Psycho* (1960).

Despite the proliferation of standardised film scores there were also attempts being made by some directors and composers to move away from standardisation. Marks notes how some *auteur* directors used film scores which differed from the norms of Hollywood; these were directors who had direct control over their work and trust in their composers who were willing to take risks. This included directors working in Hollywood such as Hitchcock, Orson Welles, Otto Preminger, William Wyler and also those working in Europe such as Michael Powell and Emeric Pressburger, Max Ophuls, and Federico Fellini (1996: 258). Some films directed by Luis Buñuel and Ingmar Bergman chose to dispense with music altogether; others used very simple music for soloists, a way of saving money and either suggesting a specific locale or providing a poignant atmosphere; for example, the use of the zither in *The Third Man* (Carol Reed, 1949) (1996b: 258). The Russian director Eisenstein focused on the musical notion of counterpoint as the central aesthetic element in his films. The musical soundtrack became vital in the construction of the narrative and when counterpoint was applied to montage it created conflict at every level (Lack 1997: 72).

Whilst the classical score had its roots firmly in late romanticism it was able to adapt and use other musical idioms, such as those of jazz and other forms of popular music. The 1940s saw the introduction of the theme score with David Raksin's score for *Laura* (Otto Preminger, 1944) being the paradigmatic example. The theme score is an approach to film scoring, which privileges a single musical theme and is often discussed in terms of opposition to classical scoring. Kalinak suggests that rather than it being a departure from the classical model, the theme score is a variation of it, using the theme in exactly the same way the classical score used leit-motifs – to provide coherence for a string of discontinuous musical cues (1992: 170). Whilst Royal S. Brown suggests that the title music for *Laura* has strong roots in the melodic and rhythmic traditions of popular music (1994: 89). The theme song from *Laura* was hugely popular and a success in its own right, this led to the theme score becoming more popular in the

1950s, with theme songs being composed specifically for the film rather than derived from the film score.

The 1940s and 1950s saw examples of *atonal** music featuring in the work of composers such as Herrmann, Miklós Rózsa, Leonard Rosenman and Jerry Goldsmith. Electronic instruments, such as the theremin and the ondes martenot also began to be used in film scores. The theremin was used by Herrmann in *Spellbound* (Alfred Hitchcock, 1945) and in *The Day the Earth Stood Still* (Robert Wise, 1951); it was also used in many 1950s science fiction films. Whilst the soundtrack to *Forbidden Planet* (Fred M. Wilcox, 1956) featured the first all-electronic film score by Louis and Bebe Barron, at the same time *discordant** sounds made their way into films with Rosenman's score for *East of Eden* (Elia Kazan, 1955).

The 1950s saw some significant changes in Hollywood film music although the model established by classical cinema broadly remained in place. Perhaps most importantly jazz and pop elements appeared nondiegetically in the work of composers such as David Raksin and Elmer Bernstein with their work providing a bridge from the classical Hollywood era to the present. Whilst jazz had been used diegetically in film between the 1920s and 1940s, from the 1950s there was a growing acceptance of jazz as serious music in the US and there are both stylistic and economic reasons for the rise of jazz as film music.

Lack notes, 'producing jazz as a soundtrack was certainly a lot cheaper for an American or any other studio than retaining its own in-house studio orchestra and associated music departments' (1997: 199). At the beginning of the 1950s Alex North's score for *A Streetcar Named Desire* (Elia Kazan, 1951) made use of the techniques and instrumental styles of jazz. Bernstein's score for *The Man with the Golden Arm* (Otto Preminger, 1955) was one of the most highly acclaimed scores of the decade, using prominent jazz elements with a memorable opening sequence which went on to become an instrumental hit in its own right. Outside of Hollywood many of the directors of the French New Wave, including Jean-Luc Godard and François Truffaut, used jazz in the soundtracks to their films.

The use of jazz was usually narratively motivated – it was often used to establish the authenticity of geographical and historical context as well as having connotations of urban culture, otherness and decadence.[7] Bernstein has discussed his use of the jazz idiom in *The Man with the Golden Arm* saying, 'The script had a Chicago slum street, heroin, hysteria, longing, frustration, despair and finally death ... I wanted an element that would localise these emotions to our country, to a large city if possible. Ergo, – jazz' (quoted in Prendergast 1977: 109). The use of jazz in film music broke up the reliance on the leitmotif and themes and was extremely influential in the way in which pop music would be used in film in the following decades (Lack 1997: 205). Smith notes how pop music had been long thought to be unsuited to film scoring for a number of reasons:

> Classical Hollywood scores were carefully timed and edited to fit the editing rhythms and movements within the frame ... In contrast, popular musical forms were thought to impose an extrinsic and rigid structure onto the visual material of the film, one that, as Mark Evans notes, was 'unrelated to the aesthetic and emotional demands of motion pictures'. (1998: 10)

Despite this there are still many examples of the use of popular music in film prior to the 1950s and 1960s, both diegetically and nondiegetically. *The Public Enemy* (William A. Wellman, 1931) used popular music over scenes of violence, a practice influential on director Martin Scorsese and Hitchcock often used popular songs because of their familiarity to audiences. The title songs for *Laura* (score by Raksin) and *The Third Man* (score by Anton Karas) were hugely successful, as was 'Do Not Forsake Me, O My Darlin' from *High Noon* (Fred Zinnemann, 1952). In the 1950s Hollywood began to exploit rock 'n' roll: the success of *The Blackboard Jungle* (Richard Brooks, 1955), which uses the Bill Haley song 'Rock Around the Clock', led to a surge of films aimed at a youth audience and in the mid-to-late 1950s rock star Elvis Presley appeared in a number of films. It is important to realise that, as Gorbman notes,

> the danger of dwelling on the 'classical Hollywood model' of film scoring is that it might give the erroneous impression of uniformity and sameness in studio-era film music. The model must not prevent us from seeing the enormous variety of musical discourses and figures it was able to encompass. However unconventional or avant-garde a Hollywood musical score might be, the film always motivates it in conventional ways. (1987: 153)

This era saw major changes for the film industry; the emergence and dominance of the vertically integrated studio system was followed by its break-up and the move towards diversification and conglomeration. The standardisation of technology also played a major role in defining the textual conventions of the classical film score, whilst conglomeration provided opportunities for cross promotion of films and film music.

The post-classical era (1960 onwards)

This era has also seen many important developments for the film industry, with more ownership changes and a return to vertical integration, not to mention the impact of synergistic marketing practices. It has also seen major technological developments and an increasingly diverse range of music being used in films.

The end of the studio system had a significant effect upon the production of film music. The major studios no longer operated using the production line, nor did they still have full-time employees, such as composers, orchestrators, and so on. There were also signs of a more creative attitude to the sourcing of music for soundtracks, particularly among the new independent film producers; this is discussed in further detail in chapter five. The trend towards diversification and conglomeration in the entertainment industries continued, which meant companies could continue to spread their risk by creating additional 'profit centres'.

During the 1970s both the film and music industries operated as oligopolies; this decade also saw the emergence of the vertically integrated media conglomerate (Gomery 1998: 51). As a result of conglomeration many studio music divisions were taken over by larger, record conglomerates. The only studios that were able to withstand threats to their music divisions were Universal and Warner Bros. During the 1980s four companies, Warner Communications Inc. (WCI), Gulf+Western (Paramount), Disney and MCA (Universal) dominated film production and distribution, and all of these companies had diversified with interests in publishing and music. A second tier of companies also had interests in related areas: MGM/UA, Columbia and Twentieth Century Fox.

Soon a new wave of mergers began; Sony bought the CBS Record Group in 1986 and Columbia Pictures in 1989 in order to have a software library to use with its new equipment, one version of synergy. Rupert Murdoch's News Corporation bought Twentieth Century Fox in 1985, Warner Communications merged with Time Inc. in 1989 to become the world's largest media conglomerate, and Matsushita bought MCA (Universal) in 1990.

The 1990s saw smaller film companies, such as Miramax and New Line, start up their own music divisions, whilst 1993 saw Miramax bought out by Disney. Record companies have also entered the film industry; in 1994 Polygram put money into independent film productions with a number of companies including Working Title and Island Pictures.

This pattern of cross-ownership meant that during the 1980s there was a tendency for companies to cross-license and in many cases deals were done between different divisions of the same conglomerate. Lack notes how the soundtrack to the American teen film *Pretty in Pink* (Howard Deutch, 1986) contains tracks by a number of then respectably well-known artists all signed to A&M Records in the US and contrasts this with the soundtrack to a similar film from the same period, *The Breakfast Club* (John Hughes, 1985), 'that looks distinctly like a case of corporate barrel-scraping', although it did help create a hit for Simple Minds with 'Don't You Forget About Me' (1997: 219–20). Nevertheless both soundtracks were successful and led director John Hughes to start up his own record label.[8]

The move towards compiled scores in the 1980s saw the increased importance of the music supervisor. Whilst music supervisors have been around since the 1940s their role has changed in parallel with the way in which the use of music in film has changed. In the studio era the music supervisor's job included some duties currently undertaken by music editors. This changed in the late 1960s, partly due to the rising popularity of the pop soundtrack and could include producing and supervising recording sessions. By the late 1970s it became increasingly common for a music supervisor to handle the placement and copyright clearance of licensed music. The role still has no definitive meaning and can vary enormously. Music supervisors can be employed within the music division of a large entertainment conglomerate or can operate on a freelance basis; many of the first music supervisors came from the music industry. Smith outlines the role of a music supervisor, which has grown to include

> the creation of a music budget, the supervision of various licensing arrangements, the negotiation of deals with composers and songwriters, and the safeguarding of the production company's publishing interests … music supervisors also participate in a number of decisions that shape the overall concept of a score … Once the score's concept is agreed upon by the filmmaker, distributor and record company, then

the music supervisor will assist in providing suitable composers, song-writers and recording artists to match that concept. (1998: 209–10)

Those music supervisors who operate as part of a large entertainment conglomerate often benefit from having easy access to songs and artists that are part of the conglomerate. They also, because of the larger volume of films produced by the majors, often have a stronger negotiating position with respect to outside publishers and record companies (Smith 1998: 211). Those music supervisors who operate on a freelance basis are occasionally hired by studios for assistance on in-house projects, but are more commonly contracted by independent producers whose work is financed and distributed by the majors. Smith suggests that, because of their involvement with almost every aspect of a soundtrack's preparation, 'music supervisors have emerged as some of Hollywood's most important dealmakers' (1998: 228). One sign of their increasing influence is that some, such as Gary LeMel and Kathy Nelson, have gone on to become the heads of major studios' music divisions.

The year 2000 saw the merger of Time Warner with the world's biggest Internet Service Provider, AOL (America Online), the merged company thus having interests in film, music, television and publishing as well as the interests of AOL. It was thought that this merger would have a major impact on both the film and music industries giving the opportunity for audiences to download music and films via the Internet, yet the full implications of this have yet to be seen.

The emergence of both new musical instruments and developments in recording technology has also had a major impact on film music, as well as a number of financial implications. This includes the introduction of the synthesiser in the mid-1960s, multi-track recording in the 1970s and MIDI-based sampling technologies and digital technology in the 1980s. Synthesisers have replaced entire orchestras on some soundtracks; Brown notes that they have also 'opened the way for certain amateurs to score films' describing how director John Carpenter has scored or co-scored many of his films (1996: 562). The technology also offers a cheaper way for composers to work, particularly on low-budget films. In the early 1980s electronics based on computer technologies also began to be used in composing film music with the use of digital sampling and pre-programming. Electronic instruments have also become commonplace in musical ensembles and many composers, including Jerry

Goldsmith, Maurice Jarre and Henry Mancini, have composed electronic scores.

Technology has also had an impact on the overall soundtrack of a film and the relationship between music, dialogue and sound effects. Lack has described how electronic film music has 'blurred the dividing line between music and sound effects and even dialogue' (1997: 314). This link between music and sound effects is discussed further in chapter two.

Sound technology continued to develop during this era; the mid-1970s saw the introduction of the Dolby Stereo Sound System, 'the first economically viable sound system' (Sergi 1998: 159). This was followed in the early 1980s with the THX sound system developed by George Lucas; and later in the 1980s with the introduction of digital sound. Other important technological developments in this era have been the introduction of new formats; the VHS, the CD and subsequently the music video in the 1980s; followed by multi-media technologies and the Digital Video Disc (DVD). By 1994 all of the major film studios had opened interactive divisions to explore the potential the new computer-based digital technologies may offer. Many of the new multi-media technologies are interactive, offering the viewer/user the opportunity to make decisions about what they see and hear, however the choice they offer is still limited and pre-determined; this is discussed in further detail in chapter five.

The past fifteen years has seen the publication of a number of influential books which attempt to theorise film music, each of which is exemplary in its own way; however, there is an emphasis on the nondiegetic score and, with the exception of some case studies, the focus is on the classical Hollywood film. The most influential of these books are Claudia Gorbman's *Unheard Melodies* (1987), Caryl Flinn's *Strains of Utopia* (1992), Kathryn Kalinak's *Settling the Score* (1992) and Royal S. Brown's *Overtones and Undertones* (1994). Gorbman's groundbreaking study, *Unheard Melodies*, focuses on classical Hollywood film music and music in European art cinema and takes as its central premise the idea that film music is unheard. Flinn's *Strains of Utopia* investigates the ways Hollywood genre films sustained the connection between music and nostalgia, utopia and femininity. Kalinak's *Settling the Score* examines the conventions and strategies underpinning film scoring in Hollywood, and Brown's *Overtones and Undertones* traces the history of film music covering both American and European cinema. Also worthy of mention is *Twenty Four Frames Under* by Russell Lack (1997), which gives a useful history of film music describing the development of music recording and that of film technology, combined with an examination of music's emotional impact on the film audience from the early days up until the present day.

There have also been other books that have concentrated on the use of popular music in film. *Celluloid Jukebox* (edited by Jonathan Romney and Adrian Wootton, 1995), is a study of popular music and the movies since the 1950s. *The Sounds of Commerce* by Jeff Smith (1998) gives an in-depth examination of how pop music shaped film entertainment since the 1950s and also provides a history of the interaction of the popular music and Hollywood film industries. *Hearing Film* by Anahid Kassabian (2001) concentrates on compiled scores in films of the 1980s and 1990s to show how contemporary film music anchors a gendered identification process. In addition, a number of anthologies published more recently feature essays by writers from a range of disciplines including film studies and musicology, giving an eclectic approach to the subject only possible in such anthologies.[9]

In an article published in 1996 Smith questions the concept of 'unheard melodies' and describes how the notion of inaudibility has been present since the mid-1930s but has taken on renewed strength in the light of the work of theorists such as Gorbman and Flinn. Smith notes that,

> Far from being 'inaudible', film music has frequently been both noticeable and memorable, often because of the various demands placed upon it to function in ancillary markets. (1996: 230)

Smith believes the consideration of film music within its economic context raises a number of significant theoretical questions with regard to the notion of 'inaudibility'. The economic context of film music is of particular interest to Smith – in *The Sounds of Commerce* he notes how the development of title songs and soundtrack albums as economic and cultural forms has generally been ignored in film music criticism (1998: 3). When popular music has been discussed its use has often been criticised; in *Knowing the Score* (1975) Irwin Bazelon wrote:

> In recent years the influx of pop musicians and assorted rock composers has turned almost every major film into a kind of musical, with hit songs born overnight, exploited and consumed like chocolate bars melting in the mouth. (1975: 29)[10]

Smith notes how Bazelon's view, which is that held by traditional musicologists and film music scholars, suggests that pop music has no intrinsic aesthetic value and is only interesting as a sociological phenomenon. Brown has also been critical of the use of popular music in film:

> By the 1980s, cine-pop music strategies often involved slipping in as many already recorded songs as possible on to a given film's music track, generally as source music, in order to attract younger audiences and to generate audio recordings that recycled these songs on to albums billed as 'original soundtracks'. The most common venue for original songs, generally performed by popular recording stars and often totally out of synch with the mood of the film, has become long, end-credit sequences that are now a permanent fixture in the cinema. (Brown 1996: 566)

During the post-classical era the changes to film music that began in the 1950s have thus continued; contemporary film music consists of a much wider range than previously and there is far more emphasis on the marketability of the pop score. This range incorporates the traditional classical score, the use of discordant music and the use of a diverse range of popular music including pop, jazz, rock, rap and electronic music. This era has also seen the influence of crossover composers, such as Mancini, Ennio Morricone and John Barry incorporating elements of the orchestral style with elements of pop/jazz. There is also evidence of a postmodern blurring of the boundaries between the diegetic and nondiegetic use of music.[11]

The 1960s not only saw an increase in the use of popular music in film but increasingly this music replaced the traditional underscore* and was used nondiegetically. This decade also saw a new group of composers including Barry, Mancini, Burt Bacharach and Quincy Jones. These composers worked on what Smith defines as the 'pop score': 'a very specific musical and cultural formation that can be located within Hollywood scoring practices since the 1960s' (1998: 238[n]). Smith notes how in developing the formal organisation of the pop score composers largely drew on the repertory of Broadway and Tin Pan Alley music of the 1930s, 1940s and 1950s, with writers such as Irving Berlin, Cole Porter and George Gershwin the models for 1960s pop composers (1998: 7).

The sound of the large-scale, romantic orchestra declined in the 1960s and 1970s; however, the late 1970s saw a rediscovery of the epic romantic film score in the wake of John Williams' music for the *Star Wars* trilogy.[12] Kalinak sees Williams as being the major force in 'returning the classical score to its late-romantic roots and adapting the symphony orchestra of Steiner and Korngold for the modern recording studio' (1992: 188).

The 1980s saw more new composers,including Carter Burwell who scored a number of Coen Brothers films, Howard Shore who scored *Silence of the Lambs* (Jonathan Demme, 1991) and a number of Cronenberg films; and Alan Silvestri who scored *Romancing the Stone* (Robert Zemeckis, 1984) and *Back to the Future* (Robert Zemeckis, 1985). Another new composer in the 1980s was Danny Elfman; Elfman has scored numerous films, including a number directed by Tim Burton. Elfman's score for Burton's *Edward Scissorhands* (1990) is discussed in chapter two.

There have also been a number of moderately well-known composers in Europe, many of who have collaborated with particular directors. Michael Nyman is one of the most prominent British contemporary film composers; he has collaborated with director Peter Greenaway on a number of films, as well as scoring Jane Campion's *The Piano* (1993). Others include Gabriel Yared who collaborated with Jean-Jacques Beneix during the 1980s (*Moon in the Gutter*, 1983; *Betty Blue*, 1986); Jurgen Knieper who has collaborated with Wim Wenders (*The State of Things*, 1982; *Wings of Desire*, 1987); and Eric Serra who has collaborated with Luc Besson (*Subway*, 1985; *The Big Blue*, 1988).

More advanced classical techniques also began to be used increasingly widely in film scoring around 1960. This gave composers a chance to experiment; for instance Goldsmith used non-traditional 'instruments', such as aluminium mixing bowls, for his score for *Planet of the Apes* (Franklin J. Schaffner, 1968). A more discordant musical language was also being used, as in Fielding's score for *Straw Dogs* (Sam Peckinpah, 1971) and Goldsmith's score for *Chinatown* (Roman Polanski, 1974). In 1971 Walter (Wendy) Carlos composed a partly synthesised score for Stanley Kubrick's *A Clockwork Orange*, which was mixed with music from Purcell, Beethoven, Rossini and Elgar. Lack notes that the early electronic film scores are 'extended song pieces running in various reprised and remixed versions throughout the soundtrack' (1997: 316). This is the case with three scores composed by Giorgio Moroder, *American Gigolo* (Paul Schrader, 1980), *Cat People* (Paul Schrader, 1982) and to a lesser degree, *Midnight Express* (Alan Parker, 1978). As mentioned previously, John Carpenter was one of the first directors to explore the use of electronic scoring by composing for his own films such as *Halloween* (1978). Some of the most well-known electronic scores of the 1980s are those composed by Vangelis for *Chariots of Fire* (Hugh Hudson, 1981) and *Blade Runner* (Ridley Scott, 1982).

By 1960 the influence of jazz could be seen in the work of established film composers such as Barry, Mancini, Lalo Schifrin and Dave Grusin. The work of these composers is also important in the development of the pop score; Smith has noted how Barry and Mancini combine 'popular styles and song forms with the developmental forms of the orchestral score' (1998: 11). Mancini's multitheme score for *Breakfast at Tiffany's* (Blake Edwards, 1961) used the format and conventions of the typical pop album; whilst *Goldfinger* (Guy Hamilton, 1964) had a score by Barry who also co-wrote the theme song performed by Shirley Bassey. The work of Morricone is also central to the development of the pop score; Morricone began scoring films in 1961 but did not achieve a commercial breakthrough until the release of Sergio Leone's *A Fistful of Dollars* in 1964. The film was hugely successful, spurred by Morricone's hit recording of the theme song; the sequels, *For a Few Dollars More* (Sergio Leone, 1965) and *The Good, the Bad and the Ugly* (Sergio Leone, 1966) were equally successful commercially and also influential in pioneering 'the absorption of pop instrumentation into scoring practices' (Romney & Wootton 1995: 7).

The unsuitability of pop music for film scoring has been mentioned previously; and it was the success of the Beatles and *A Hard Day's Night* (Richard Lester, 1964) which encouraged the film industry and their record subsidiaries to include more popular music in film. Pop and rock groups began to appear in films, sometimes playing themselves; examples include The Monkees in *Head* (Bob Rafelson, 1968) and Alan Price in *O Lucky Man!* (Lindsay Anderson, 1973). Jean-Luc Godard also built a large portion of *Sympathy for the Devil* (1968) around a Rolling Stones song. The success of *The Graduate* (Mike Nichols, 1967) and *Easy Rider* (Dennis Hopper, 1969) was extremely important in terms of advancing the use of rock and pop songs as dramatic underscore. Whilst the use of popular music in *American Graffiti* (George Lucas, 1973) established the compilation score, a score comprised of self-contained songs which were usually prerecorded, this type of score became prevalent during the 1980s and 1990s.[13]

The late 1960s and early 1970s also saw a number of pop stars and rock musicians composing film music, this increasingly common phenomenon is discussed in further detail in chapter four. In the early 1970s blaxploitatation films used soul and funk music that inflected the background scores; whilst soundtracks such as Isaac Hayes' for *Shaft* (Gordon Parks, 1971) and Curtis Mayfield's for *Superfly* (Gordon Parks Jr., 1972) were hugely successful. Others, such as Marvin Gaye's score for *Trouble Man* (Ivan Dixon, 1972) and James Brown's for *Black Caesar* (Larry Cohen, 1973) have become cult classics. The influence of pop music on film continued with some directors using pre-existing music admirably, perhaps the best example of this being Scorsese in films such as *Mean Streets* (1973), *Alice Doesn't Live Here Anymore* (1974) and *GoodFellas* (1990). The score for *GoodFellas* is discussed in chapter two.

Scores compiled from a mix of original music, classical pieces and popular music also continued being used, perhaps most notably, in the films of the New German Cinema in the late 1970s and early 1980s, as well as in the films of Spanish director Pedro Almodóvar; these are also discussed in chapter two. The score for Anthony Minghella's 1990 film *Truly, Madly, Deeply* used a combination of music; a score composed by Barrington Pheloung, classical pieces by Bach, as well as popular music; with each of the different types of music being used for a different function. The score was described as mixing music,

> in what may at first seem an indiscriminate hodgepodge. However, most of the music was written specifically into the screenplay and is part of a rich network of symbols that operate overtly, but rarely obtrusively, throughout the film. (Stilwell 1997: 61)

In the 1990s the British film *Shopping* (Paul Anderson, 1994) used dance music; as did the opening titles of *Shallow Grave* (Danny Boyle, 1994). *Trainspotting* (Danny Boyle, 1996) was one of a number of films that used dance music to signify the change in culture brought about at the turn of the 1990s. By the end of the 1990s, films such as *Greenwich Mean Time* (John Strickland, 1999) and *Human Traffic* (Justin Kerrigan, 1999) were based wholly on the new dance music and club culture. DJs such as Paul Oakenfold and Dave Pearce have also become involved in film, both having worked as music supervisors; Pearce on *South West 9* (Richard Parry, 2001) and Oakenfold on *Swordfish* (Dominic Sena, 2001).

Kalinak has suggested that the use of jazz and pop idioms challenged the Hollywood score but did not subvert it altogether (1992: 184–8). In the new millennium there are still a large number of successful American composers writing large-scale symphonic soundtracks, examples include Howard Shore, Thomas Newman and James Horner. Smith suggests that contemporary film scores generally fit into one of four basic stylistic models each with its own appropriate pattern of thematic organisation: (i) letimotif-laden orchestral scores composed within neo-romantic or *modernist** styles; (ii) orchestral scores that feature one or two popular songs; (iii) scores comprised entirely of popular recordings; (iv) scores that mix orchestral underscore with several pop tunes (1998: 215). Consideration of Smith's models would appear to suggest that the Hollywood score continues to be subverted with more and more films using popular music in some way.

This era has thus seen many changes in film music, and by the end of the millennium classical film music was still being composed but was only one variant among many. Different genres of popular music have been used in film, both diegetically and nondiegetically, and compiled, rather than composed, scores have grown in popularity leading to the high-profile role of the music supervisor and the increased importance of cross-promotional strategies. These factors have had a major effect on the film and music industries and the marketing of both films and soundtrack albums. Furthermore, the effects of digital technology are being felt throughout the film industry – in production, distribution and exhibition – and the threat of digital piracy is a major concern for the film industry, as it has been for the music industry.

This chapter has outlined the development of film music in three eras, considering how industry organisation and technology has affected film music, as well as exploring critical attitudes to film music and outlining the textual conventions during each era. Whilst there have been numerous changes in each of the areas discussed what is clear is that there are also a number of practices which have continued since the early days of film through to the new millennium. Three major themes have been established; firstly, the prevalence of popular music and its perceived inferiority; secondly, that of the perceived superiority of the original score; and thirdly, the use of music as a marketing tool, each of which will be drawn on throughout the book.

2   TEXTUAL FUNCTIONS OF FILM MUSIC

Following on from chapter one which outlined the textual conventions of film music this chapter will concentrate on the textual functions of film music. The chapter begins with a summary of some of the key theoretical work that has been done, focusing firstly on the functions of music in the classical Hollywood film and including an in-depth discussion of Danny Elfman's original classical score for *Edward Scissorhands*. There is then discussion of the functions of music in scores compiled from popular music. This is followed by two case studies, the first discussing the *composite**** scores used by two European directors, Rainer Werner Fassbinder and Pedro Almodóvar, the second discussing the score for Martin Scorsese's *GoodFellas*, comprised entirely of prerecorded popular music.[1]

Before discussing the functions of music in film it is necessary to briefly outline music's role in the overall soundtrack of a film. Soundtracks are comprised of three basic components of dialogue, sound effects and music and the effectiveness of any music used is determined by its place in the soundtrack.[2] Much early writing on film music was of the idea that the music should be subordinated to the voice, remaining in the background and 'unheard' and it is only in recent years that the audible quality of film music has been recognised.[3] Annahid Kassabian discusses how music interacts with other aspects of the scene and how much attention viewers/listeners give to the music in comparison to the dialogue, visuals and other elements. She outlines an 'Attention Continuum', making the point that theme songs are generally given a lot of audience attention; scenes with an absence of anything besides music on the soundtrack also focus attention onto the music. Next on the continuum is music with very little competition from other sounds, which are there but have a low profile in comparison to the music. Further along are scenes in which there is a lot of visual action, usually with both sound effects and music, but little or no dialogue; and finally music commands the least attention when it is used as background to dialogue (2001: 52–4).

As mentioned in chapter one, the introduction of electronic film music blurred the dividing line between music, sound effects and dialogue and since the 1970s there have been examples of sound effects used as music and music used as sound effect. An example of this is editor and sound designer Walter Murch's use of helicopters as the 'string section' in the orchestra in *Apocalypse Now* (1979). In a more recent article Kassabian explores 'the evaporating boundaries and hierarchies between sound and music'; discussing how, 'distinctions between foreground and background sound are slowly disappearing and, with them, the distinctions among noise, sound and music' (2003: 140). To demonstrate her argument she discusses the use of sound in *The Cell* (Tarsem Singh, 2000) saying, 'This is neither music nor not music, but rather a textural use of sound that disregards most, if not all, of the "laws" of classic Hollywood film-scoring technique' (2003: 143). This is an interesting development worthy of further discussion, which is outside of the scope of this book. However, it is important to realise that music is just one element of the soundtrack and that the dividing lines between all three elements are becoming increasingly blurred.

The functions of music in the classical Hollywood film

A number of writers and composers have discussed the functions of music in the classical film.[4] In 1949 the composer Aaron Copland offered a useful summary of the functions of music in film by suggesting five general areas in which film music serves the screen: (i) it conveys a convincing atmosphere of time and place; (ii) it underlines the unspoken feelings or psychological states of characters; (iii) it serves as a kind of neutral background filler to the action; (iv) it gives a sense of continuity to the editing; (v) it accentuates the theatrical build-up of a scene and rounds it off with a feeling of finality (Smith 1998: 6).

The most influential writing in this area has been Claudia Gorbman's book *Unheard Melodies*. The book discusses how music signifies in films not only according to pure musical codes, but also according to cultural musical codes and the cinematic musical codes of beginning- and end-title music, and musical themes (1987: 2–3). Gorbman also identifies seven principles of the composition, mixing and editing of music in classical film and strongly argues the case for the music being subordinated to the narrative. However, 'ultimately it is the narrative context, the interrelations between music and the rest of the film's system, that determines the effectiveness of film music' (1987: 12). Each element of Copland's list reappears in Gorbman's seven principles, which are as follows:

(i)   *invisibility*: the technical apparatus of nondiegetic music must not be visible.
(ii) *inaudibility*: music is not meant to be heard consciously. As such it should subordinate itself to dialogue, to visuals, that is, to the primary vehicles of the narrative.
(iii) *signifier of emotion*: soundtrack music may set specific moods and emphasise particular emotions suggested in the narrative, but first and foremost, it is a signifier of emotion itself.
(iv) *narrative cueing*: (a) *referential/narrative* – music gives referential and narrative cues, for example indicating point of view, supplying formal demarcations and establishing setting and characters; (b) *connotative* – music 'interprets' and 'illustrates' narrative events.
(v)   *continuity*: music provides formal and rhythmic continuity – between shots, in transitions between scenes, by filling 'gaps'.
(vi) *unity*: via repetition and variation of musical material and instrumentation, music aids in the construction of formal and narrative unity.
(vii) a given film score may violate any of the principles above, providing the violation is at the service of other principles (1987: 73).

It is Gorbman's second point about the 'inaudibility' of film music that is perhaps the most problematic and worthy of further discussion. Gorbman clarifies her use of the term:

> I have set the term in quotes because, of course, film music can always be heard. However … a set of conventional practices has evolved which result in the spectator not normally hearing it or attending to it consciously. (1987: 76)

Gorbman goes on to outline some practices dictated by the principle of inaudibility. Firstly, musical form is generally determined by or subordinated to narrative form; secondly, music should be subordinated to the voice; thirdly, for editing certain points are 'better' than others at which music may stop or start, thus music almost never enters simultaneously with the entrance of a voice on the soundtrack as it would drown out the words; and fourthly, the music's mood must be appropriate to the scene, the point being to provide a musical parallel to the action to reinforce the mood.[5]

As mentioned in chapter one, most of the writing on film music has concentrated on nondiegetic music. Gorbman makes the important point that critics often make the error of classifying music as either nondiegetic and therefore capable of expression; or diegetic and thus divorced from the task of articulating moods and dramatic tensions.[6] Gorbman argues that diegetic music also has an affective role:

> The mood of any music on the soundtrack, be it diegetic or nondi-egetic music, will be felt in association with diegetic events ... the special expressive effect of diegetic music is its capacity to create irony, in a more 'natural' way than nondiegetic music. (1987: 23)

The affective role of diegetic music is discussed in the case studies later in this chapter. As there has been a great deal written about the functions of music in the classical Hollywood film I have chosen here to use an example of an original classical score for a contemporary Hollywood film: Danny Elfman's original score for *Edward Scissorhands*.

Elfman is completely self-taught as a composer and was a member of rock band Oingo Boingo in the late 1970s and early 1980s before being hired to score Tim Burton's first feature, *Pee-Wee's Big Adventure* in 1985. After scoring Burton's *Batman* in 1989 he became hugely successful and went on to score other films for Burton and for other directors.[7] Elfman's work is reminiscent of that of composers such as Steiner and Korngold with his use of leitmotifs, mickey-mousing and a large orchestra.[8]

Edward Scissorhands was Burton's fourth feature film and tells the story of a man-made creation, whose inventor died before he was finished, leaving him with scissors for hands. He is rescued from his existence in the castle on the hill by Peg Boggs, the local Avon lady who takes him to live with her family in the suburban town. Edward is attracted to Kim, the Boggs's daughter and jealous of her relationship with boyfriend Jim; mean-while his appearance makes him a novelty in the neighbourhood and his topiary and hair-cutting skills make him popular with the neighbours. As the film progresses events occur and feelings change towards Edward; and the end of the film returns him to solitude in the castle on the hill. Elfman has said that the score to *Edward Scissorhands* is one of his favourites, noting how it taps into his love of film scores of the 1930s and 1940s, which is all about storytelling through music (DVD commentary).

Here we will explore how Elfman's score operates as a integral part of the film text working with other elements of the *mise-en-scène* to perfectly match the sense of melancholic tragedy and childhood innocence. Elfman describes how the music playing over the extended title sequence of the film is important in terms of setting the scene and giving the audience an idea of what they are about to see and feel (DVD commentary). The music in this sequence is divided into three parts. The first is Edward's first theme emphasising the playful, fairytale side of Edward; this plays over the opening credits of the film, which are dark but playful at the same time. The second is the storytime theme, which plays over the scene of the grandmother telling the bedtime story, reflecting the warm, homely look of the images. The third part is Edward's second theme, using the choir, which emphasises his emotional side and the heart of his character; this begins as the camera tracks across the town and up into the castle on the hill. Both the opening music and the images emphasise the fairytale quality of the film, which moves between the extremes of delight and dread.

The entire opening theme is played very darkly as Peg enters the castle. During this sequence the music changes to reflect Peg's changing feelings; as she explores the castle and its surroundings she expresses wonder at the beautiful gardens with their flowers and topiary, and the frolicking music reflects this. As Peg knocks on the door of the castle the music becomes more ominous reflecting her sense of foreboding, as she goes inside the castle and looks around seeing the hole in the roof and the press cuttings on the wall, before she comes face to face with Edward for the first time. The music perfectly complements the images, emphasising the ordinariness of Peg and the extraordinariness of Edward and again reflects the two extremes of the film which moves from being a pleasant fairytale to becoming dark and menacing.

Once Peg decides to take Edward home with her the suburbia theme reflects Edward's wonder and excitement at seeing the outside world for the first time, and this works well with the pastel-coloured houses. When Peg is showing Edward around the Boggs household a subtle variation of

Edward's main theme is heard as he enters a room and walks over to look at the family photographs. The music becomes more romantic as Edward stands awestruck and smiles as the camera pans around and closes in on photographs of Kim as Peg says, 'Isn't she beautiful?' The music for the 'Cookie Factory' scene is quirky and upbeat, using mickey-mousing to give a tempo to the machinery and reflecting the inventor's sense of excitement. The emphasis is very much on the music and images as there is no dialogue during this scene. The scene ends with the inventor having the idea of turning the machine into a boy, and as he picks up a heart-shaped cookie the music changes to become more thoughtful and reflective. The music is also an extremely important supportive element of the *mise-en-scène* during the hair-cutting sequence. Joyce, one of the neighbours who is attracted to Edward, has admired his topiary work and dog clipping and asks him to cut her hair. Edward agrees and as he cuts her hair she is seen curling her toes orgasmically, her facial expression one of blissful ecstasy, whilst Edward is shown in deep concentration. Edward then cuts the hair of some of the other women as the music becomes more dramatic with some quirky violin playing. Elfman discusses writing this scene and responding to the state of ecstasy the women were in in the chair, saying that Edward was, 'using the quality the women saw in him. He was really making love to them wasn't he?' (DVD commentary). The turning point in the film occurs when Edward appears on the television show; it is at this point that Kim begins defending Edward rather than being turned off by him, and this is emphasised by a brief statement of Edward's theme. Shortly after this both the music and the images change to become darker and more menacing, as the earlier musical themes are inverted to reflect suburbia's changing feelings towards Edward. Elfman discusses how the innocent and tender themes from earlier in the film are changing but he is still trying to keep a melodic thread through the music, so that even though the tone of the film has changed the melody keeps it all together.

For Elfman 'The Ice Dance' sequence was always a major focus, defining the beginning and ending of the film and epitomising the heart of the score (DVD commentary). The scene takes place at Christmas as Edward is working outside on an ice sculpture that creates snow. The sculpture is in the shape of an angel and as Edward sculpts, Kim dances; this is an enchanting, dream-like scene, which reflects the fairytale element of the film. Again there is no dialogue and the emphasis is very much on Elfman's music to tell the story. The images match the music with Kim look-

FIGURE 1 *Edward Scissorhands* (Tim Burton, 1990)

ing angelic; she is wearing a white dress emphasising her innocence and her facial expression is one of blissful happiness. This scene ends abruptly as Jim appears and Edward accidentally cuts Kim with his hands, and the music becomes more dramatic and menacing. This leads into the rampage scene as Edward walks off having rowed with Jim. Edward cuts off his own clothes, destroys his topiary and slashes car tyres, the music reflecting his sense of frustration.

Elfman's score is used nondiegetically and follows Gorbman's principles of film scoring in the classical Hollywood film. The music signifies emotions with Edward's two themes reflecting his emotional states; it works to establish setting and characters as well as to interpret and illustrate narrative events; and also provides unity as the tone of the film changes.

The functions of music in scores compiled from popular music

Until the 1960s the nondiegetic score was commonly orchestral, but the diegetic score has always consisted mainly of popular song. The increasing use of popular songs as nondiegetic music has now become commonplace in films from *The Graduate* and *Easy Rider* to *Billy Elliot* (Stephen Daldry, 2000) and *The Royal Tenenbaums* (Wes Anderson, 2001). This has led to distinctions being made between the supposed 'high culture' of the orchestral score and the supposed 'low culture' of the pop score.

It was not until 1998 and the publication of Jeff Smith's book, *The Sounds of Commerce*, that the use of music in compiled as opposed to composed scores was considered. Discussing the dramatic functions of the compiled score, Smith comments on how individual songs are typically used in ways not unlike the cues of the conventional orchestral score; songs are *spotted** so that they may perform any or all of the classical score's traditional functions – including establishing mood and supporting the film's construction of formal unity. For Smith the main difference between the two being the way in which the compilation score has a tendency to emphasise certain functions over others:

> Because of its formal autonomy, the compilation score is much less likely to be used as an element of structural and rhythmic continuity. Instead, filmmakers frequently use songs as a way of establishing mood and setting, and as a commentary on the film's characters and action. (1998: 155)

Others have pointed out the problems with using pop songs as score, Kathryn Kalinak notes that the use of pop songs posed formal difficulties because of the song's structural unity and integrity, believing that because these songs cannot be segmented in the same way as themes or leitmotifs pop/rock scores ignore certain fundamental principles at the heart of the classical score. These principles include the use of music to illustrate narrative content; to provide structural unity; and as an inaudible component of narrative signification. Kalinak believes rock music committed the cardinal sin of film scoring – it failed to support the story and mood because it *was* the story and mood (Kalinak 1992: 186–7; see also Smith 1998: 164).

Another potential problem with regard to how pop songs function in films is the fact that pop songs are usually chosen for a film rather than specifically composed for it. As Smith notes:

> As such, these scores broke with a long-standing taboo in Hollywood scoring against using well-known music ... Well-known music of any kind was thought to carry associational baggage for

the spectator, and not only was this potentially distracting but these associations might also clash with those established by the narrative. (1998: 164)

As discussed in chapter one, many of the early scores did in fact use well-known music; however, this only appears to have been seen as problematic with the increasing use of popular songs as nondiegetic music from the 1960s. A number of filmmakers and composers have chosen to deal with the problem of popular songs being chosen for a film rather than specifically composed for it by shooting and editing to the selected pop songs rather than adding the songs in post-production. A case study of *The Big Chill* (Lawrence Kasdan, 1983) discusses how the film was cut to the song track, to achieve the traditional relationship between movement (action) and musical rhythm and texture (Carey & Hannan 2003: 268).

In the afterword to *Unheard Melodies* Gorbman asks if the use of popular music in 1980s films is really different in kind from its use in the traditional Hollywood musical, where it is a matter of convention for the flow and space of the narrative to be disrupted by a musical number (1987: 162). The use of songs with lyrics is also problematic, and Gorbman discusses how songs require narrative to cede to spectacle, as it seems that lyrics and action compete for attention. She uses examples from dramatic films, such as *Gilda* (Charles Vidor, 1946), where a character sings a song, stating that the action necessarily freezes for the duration of the song, to back up her point. Gorbman states that the same is true for songs sung nondiegetically, heard over the film's images, as in *Rancho Notorious* (Fritz Lang, 1952):

Rather than participating in the action, these theme songs behave somewhat like a Greek chorus, commenting on a narrative temporarily frozen into spectacle. (1987: 19–20)[9]

Meanwhile Royal S. Brown argues that song lyrics threaten to offset the aesthetic balance between music and narrative cinematic representation and that the common solution taken by the standard feature film is not to declare songs off-limits – for they can give pleasure of their own – but to defer significant action and dialogue during their performance (1994: 20).

Two recent essays have compared the use of popular music in film to that of classical music and demonstrate that many of the perceived problems can also be advantageous. Melissa Carey and Michael Hannan's essay on *The Big Chill* discusses how the lyrics, rather than disturbing the balance between music and narrative, bring an enhanced level of intertextuality to the soundtrack and supply a self-sufficient narrative allowing for a more abstract visual treatment (2003: 268). Lauren Anderson analyses the use of music in the British film *Sliding Doors* (Peter Howitt, 1998) and a New Zealand film, *Topless Women Talk About Their Lives* (Harry Sinclair, 1997). She concludes that popular music can be used to fulfill functions traditionally carried out by a 'classical' composed film score but that it does this in slightly different ways to 'classical' film music. Further, Anderson points out that the compilation score draws on some features particular to popular music: in particular, (i) the lyrics, (ii) the songs' structural independence, and (iii) the extra-textual meanings conveyed by the songs (2003: 168–9). The lyrics seem to play the most important part, having direct links to the songs' structural independence and to the extra-textual meanings. Smith mentions how the lyrics of popular music proffer a kind of double-edged sword, 'Indeed they carry a certain potential for distraction, but their referential dimension can also be exploited to "speak for" characters or comment on a film's action' (1998: 166). Anderson uses Smith to comment on how it is the lyrics that usually give referential meaning to music, and that, 'unlike "classical" film music's subordination to dialogue, popular music's lyrics can replace or substitute for dialogue' (2003: 169).

Whilst Smith has stated that popular music is much less likely to be used as an element of structural and rhythmic continuity, Anderson's useful counter-example demonstrates how her two examples show that popular music can be used to maintain continuity and unity, though reduction to short themes or leitmotifs is not necessarily required to achieve this, indicating that popular music is not necessarily as limited in its potential for formal use as Smith has suggested (2003: 171).

The extra-textual meanings are also often related to the song lyrics as well as conveying a sense of the social and historical context. Because of the compilation score's heavy reliance on pop and rock tunes, its meaning within a film is often dependent upon the meaning of pop music in the larger spheres of society and culture (Smith 1995: 155).

In addition to the functions of classical music in film it seems that popular music in film has some specific functions to perform, these, following Smith, can be summarised as follows:

- as an effective means of denoting particular time periods (1998: 165);
- to highlight the element of authorial expressivity by commenting *on* characters rather than speaking from their point of view (1998: 169);
- the lyrics can give voice to feelings and attitudes not made explicit by the film's visuals and dialogue (1998: 170);
- intertextual/extra-textual/musical allusionism can be used to flesh-out characters, and emphasise particular generic or narrative themes (ibid.).

Both the functions outlined here by Gorbman and by Smith will be used in the case studies in the next part of this chapter.

Case Study: the composite scores used by Fassbinder and Almodóvar

In this section we shall consider the use of music in films made outside of Hollywood and explore how music is used in the work of two European directors, Rainer Werner Fassbinder and Pedro Almodóvar. There are a number of similarities between the two; of most relevance is that both directors have used the melodramatic form in a number of their films and both have used composite scores comprised of original music, pre-existing classical pieces and popular songs. Gorbman's theory of film music will be used here, as many of the films she used as examples were melodramas from the classical Hollywood era. This section will consider how music operates in the contemporary melodramas of these two directors and how it opposes Gorbman's theory in a number of ways. There will be a focus on the range of music used and an exploration of the use of popular song as an integral part of the narrative, as well as consideration of the cultural connotations of the music.

Fassbinder was one of the most significant and prolific directors of the New German Cinema of the 1970s and 1980s. He worked in theatre before making his first film, *Love is Colder than Death*, in 1969. Fassbinder's versatility meant that as well as directing he also wrote scripts, took on acting roles, worked as an editor, producer and production designer and also composed music for his own films. By the time of his premature death from a drug-related overdose in 1982 he had directed over forty films. Fassbinder frequently worked with a group of tightly-knit collaborators, one of whom was composer Peer Raben; Raben's work with Fassbinder included composing for the films and also the choice of pre-existing music.

Pedro Almodóvar is one of Spain's most internationally acclaimed contemporary film directors. In the 1970s he became part of Madrid's pop subculture acting in avant-garde theatre groups and performing in drag in a punk rock band. His first feature film, *Pepi, Luci, Bom y otras chicas* (1980), became a cult hit and with later films his work has become acknowledged internationally. The music for Almodóvar's early films tended to be an eclectic bricolage whereas the later work features commissioned musical scores by composers such as Bernardo Bonezzi (*Matador*, 1986; *Women on the Verge of a Nervous Breakdown*, 1988); Ennio Morricone (*Tie Me Up! Tie Me Down!*, 1990); Ryuichi Sakamoto (*High Heels*, 1991); and Alberto Iglesias (*Flower of My Secret*, 1995 onwards).

In her study of music in the classical Hollywood film Gorbman refers to Steiner as 'surely one of the most melodramatic of Hollywood's great film composers', going on to say that she uses Steiner's music to illustrate the model of classical scoring outlined earlier because 'fundamentally, the classical Hollywood film *is* melodrama – a drama with music' (1987: 7). The tradition of music accompanying drama has been present for hundreds of years, returning to popularity in the late eighteenth century and continued through nineteenth century forms of popular entertainment and into the world of film. Gorbman describes how 'melodrama called for music to mark entrances of characters, to provide interludes, and to give emotional colouring to dramatic climaxes and to scenes with rapid physical action' (1987: 34).

Fassbinder was influenced by the Hollywood melodrama, in particular the work of director Douglas Sirk and a number of his films draw upon the conventions of melodrama. The film that brought him international acclaim, *Fear Eats the Soul* (1974), bears a number of similarities to Sirk's *All That Heaven Allows* (1955), using dramatic excess to push events to extremes. The work of Almodóvar also shows the influence of Sirk; this is particularly the case with *High Heels,* where Sirk's influence can be seen in the distinctive *mise-en-scène*, the use of colours and music. The term 'excessive' has been frequently used to describe the work of Sirk, Fassbinder and Almodóvar. Geoffrey Nowell-Smith discusses how in melodrama the laying out of the problems 'realistically' always allow for the generating of an excess which cannot be accommodated:

> The undischarged emotion which cannot be accommodated within
> the action ... is traditionally expressed in the music and, in the

case of film, in certain elements of the *mise-en-scène*. That is to say, music and *mise-en-scène* do not just heighten the emotionality of an element of the action: to some extent they substitute for it. (1987: 73)

Music is central to the excesses of melodrama and those of New German Cinema. Caryl Flinn notes the role of the past in shaping the present, with

the repressed traumas revealing themselves only in highly displaced non-linguistic ways (aphasic conditions, Sirkian colours and scores by Max Steiner). (1994: 107)

Music has a conspicuous role in the films of the New German Cinema with films often using a combination of original pieces, popular songs and quotations from earlier classical pieces. It is this combination of music, which differentiates the use of music in these films from that of the classical Hollywood model and in so doing opposes one of Gorbman's points that music is used to reinforce unity (1987: 73). Flinn has described how,

During the 1970s and early 1980s, the young German cinema freely pillaged existing music, which it then put to different uses. One of the interesting features of this extended culture raid is its refusal of stylistic unity: meshed musical styles of film soundtracks of the time are quite common. (Flinn 2000: 128)

Whilst this combination of music is certainly not new, in many of Fassbinder's films, and also a number of Almodóvar's, it is the sheer range of music used, the way in which it is used, and often its repetition, which leads to the overall feeling of excess. The score for *The Marriage of Maria Braun* (1979) includes pieces by Beethoven and Mozart, an extract from the opera *Der Rosenkavalier* and Raben's original score. The beginning of this film also demonstrates an interesting mix of sound effects and music as Beethoven's Ninth Symphony is played amongst the chaos of bombs falling and windows smashing, with the music being barely audible. The piece continues into another scene in which it is even quieter; in this scene it is being played diegetically on the radio. Music plays a major role in *Lili Marleen* (1981), which is subtitled 'the story of a song', the title song being repeated on numerous occasions throughout the film. As well as this the film also uses a classical piece by Mahler and a score by Raben. *Veronika Voss* (1982) uses a Bruch violin concerto, and a number of American popular songs as well as Raben's score.

Composer Peer Raben has also highlighted music's intertextual, 'borrowed' role, maintaining that, '*all* styles of music from *all* periods can accompany *any* story of *any* period. Film music should aim for what he calls an "additive originality"' (Flinn 1994: 110). This is another difference between the use of music in these films and in the classical Hollywood film and opposes another of Gorbman's points that, 'the music's mood must be appropriate to the scene' (1987: 78). Roger Hillman has noted how, even though many of Fassbinder's films overlap with Gorbman's concerns, in *The Marriage of Maria Braun*,

> the subtle musical aspect of the melodrama surrounding Maria Braun transcends any of the models offered by Gorbman's material. Music is not just an adjunct to the camera, opening up the linear representation of narrative time when it 'accompanies montage and slow motion sequences, imitates flashbacks and so on'. (1995: 191)

In this case the soundtrack undermines the visual level rather than supports it. This opposes Gorbman's point that 'narrative film music "anchors" the image in meaning' (1987: 84).

Almodóvar has also used a range of music in his films, including music from films by other directors as well as the recycling of music and songs in his own films.[10] *Kika* (1993) has a score of non-original music, including an extract of Herrmann's score from *Psycho*; *Women on the Verge of a Nervous Breakdown* includes a score by Bonezzi as well as classical pieces by Rimsky-Korsakov; whilst *High Heels* includes Sakamoto's score and music by Miles Davis as well as a number of boleros. In Almodóvar's films the bolero, a sentimental song or ballad which originated in Latin America, has been used as a narrative device. José Arroyo notes, 'The bolero can not only "contain" excess, it demands it' (1992: 39). At times the bolero appears nondiegetically, at other times it is performed by characters within the film; in both cases, with its excessive sentimentality, it could be perceived as absurd, however this is not the case when the story being told is a melodrama.

Let us consider Gorbman's theory that action stops for the performance of songs in dramatic films, as many of the films made by these two directors feature characters performing songs. Gorbman suggests that 'Songs require narrative to cede to spectacle, for it seems that lyrics and action compete for attention' (1987: 20). In Fassbinder's films there are examples from *Lili Marleen* which demonstrate that narrative does in fact cede to spectacle. As previously mentioned, the title song is repeated on numerous occasions in the film and is often performed. Hillman notes how these performances work to

> momentarily halt not just the immediate dramatic action but, according to the film's conceit, the world-stage of conflict, as soldiers from both sides listen in thrall to its regular evening broadcast. (2001)

Whilst many films do demonstrate that narrative cedes to spectacle there are also exceptions to this. *Veronika Voss* features a song performed by the main character. There is also an element of repetition here as the song, 'Memories', is heard a number of times. It is first heard diegetically as Veronika plays the piano and sings a refrain whilst in her house with the journalist Robert; it is then heard playing diegetically on the radio in the clinic. Towards the end of the film Veronika performs the song with piano accompaniment watched by the other characters in the film. The lyrics play an important role in the narrative and read like a recipe for a love affair:

> Take one fresh and tender kiss
> Add one stolen night of bliss
> One girl one boy
> Some grief some joy
> Memories are made of this

The lyrics of the song throughout stress the importance of 'memories' being 'the dreams you will savour'; memories are all that Veronika has left. Rather than significant action and dialogue being deferred during the performance the lyrics themselves work as significant dialogue.

Songs play a major part in the narrative of Almodóvar's films, often speaking for the characters, with no additional voice-over or dialogue. In both *Law of Desire* and *Women on the Verge of a Nervous Breakdown*, two boleros tell much of the story of the emotions and relationships between the characters.

This is also the case in *High Heels* – the story of Rebecca, the daughter of ex-actress Becky and wife of Manuel, her mother's ex-lover. The three, along with Lethal, a drag artist who impersonates Becky in her earlier years, are the main characters. The film features a number of boleros, Femme Lethal performs the first of these in the club as part of his act as 'The real Becky'. The lyrics read:

> You'll recall the happiness we shared
> You'll recall the taste of my kisses

As Lethal sings the other three main characters, Rebecca, Becky and Manuel exchange looks, all three reminded of past events by the lyrics. This is confirmed when Manuel says to Becky, 'Didn't that song bring back memories?' to which she replies, 'Too many.'

The second bolero in the film is first heard as Becky is seen on stage on her return to Madrid; she dedicates the song to Rebecca who is in prison. This live performance of 'Piensa en mí' ('Think of Me') is fully integrated into the narrative. The performance is being broadcast on the radio and Rebecca hears her mother singing,

> If your heart is breaking
> Think of me
> If you feel like crying
> Think of me
> You know I adore your divine image

The performance is intercut with images of Rebecca, lying on her prison bed crying, and of the audience watching Becky perform. There is an element of repetition here as the opening verse of this bolero is heard again when Lethal returns to play at the club and sings it to Rebecca after her release from prison; again it is performed but this time with Lethal sitting at a table with Rebecca. In both of these cases the lyrics are fully integrated into the narrative and the performance does not cede to spectacle.

Gorbman notes how music, as something not consciously perceived, can inflect the narrative with emotive values via cultural musical codes (1987: 4). The use of music in the films of these two directors has interesting cultural connotations relating to both national cultures and the high/ low culture debate. The use of Arabic music in Fassbinder's *Fear Eats the*

FIGURE 2 *High Heels* (Pedro Almodóvar, 1991)

Soul works to suggest the outsider status of the 'Gastarbeiter' in German society as well as suggest a blurring of cultural and national identities. This is also the case with the American popular songs used in *Veronika Voss*; they also reflect one of the major concerns of the New German Cinema, the influence of American culture on post-war Germany. During the majority of the scenes that take place in the clinic of the neurologist treating Veronika Voss, American country and western music is heard. This generally seems to be playing diegetically from a radio and whilst the volume varies and the lyrics cannot always be heard; the lyrics of two songs stand out. The first, with its refrain of 'Down the Mississippi to the Gulf of Mexico', has geographical connotations of America. Whilst the second, with its refrain of 'I owe my soul to the company store', connotes the dependence of both the elderly couple who are survivors of Treblinka and also of Veronika, on American supplies of morphine.[11]

Mark Allinson has noted in Almodóvar's films that,

> sometimes music is chosen more for its specific, cultural or intertextual associations rather than its quality or tone. Among such associations are those of national identity, religion, popular culture and other films. In the early films in particular, Almodóvar plays with questions of national identity in his choice of music. (2001: 197)

The soundtrack to *All About my Mother* (1999), another Almodóvar melodrama, has one track titled 'All About Eve' and another titled 'Just Like Eve Harrington' both references to the Joseph L. Mankiewicz film, *All About Eve* from 1950. Whilst another track, 'Dedicatoria', plays as Almodóvar pays homage to all actresses who have played actresses.

Fassbinder's *The Marriage of Maria Braun* uses Beethoven and Mozart as a testament of high, official German culture. *Lili Marleen* uses both popular and classical music to flesh out details of the two main characters. One example is from the latter part of the film as Robert conducts Mahler's Eighth Symphony – this can be seen as an example of music as a form of high culture in contrast to the low culture of the popular song 'Lili Marleen' with which Willie is identified throughout the film. Meanwhile Allinson suggests that Almodóvar's main reason for using classical pieces in his films is an economic one, as the rights are either free or cheap to obtain (2001: 195).

Whilst the music in these films does perform some of the functions of music in the classical Hollywood film as identified by Gorbman, in other ways it opposes some of these principles. The reasons for this are complex. However, one important factor is that as well as using narrative devices common to the melodrama, both directors also use the devices of art cinema, and in so doing, subvert the genre of melodrama. The use of a diverse range of music in the films of both of these directors transcends the boundaries of classical film scoring with each element of the music performing different functions and thus subverting the way in which music is used in the classical Hollywood melodrama. The increased use of popular song is important here, particularly when it is used as an integral part of the narrative. Gorbman's point about the affective role of diegetic music is also significant: whilst music used nondiegetically can only affect the audience, diegetic music also has an effect on the characters. In many of the examples used here the songs have a dramatic emotional effect on the characters, which often leads to a feeling of excess.

Although the idea of a composite score is not new and goes back as far as D. W. Griffith's *The Birth of a Nation* in 1915, these examples emphasise the fact that, particularly outside of Hollywood, a diverse range of music is being used in non-standardised ways. This inevitably leads to a blurring of the boundaries between high and low culture as well as reflecting the changing needs of audiences. This is also reflected in the films themselves, which show a merging of the mass art form of the melodrama with the high art form of the European art film. The films are seen internationally as a product of high culture and shown in art-house cinemas, whereas the music used blurs the boundaries between high and low. These examples show it is still possible for composite scores to perform the functions of film music outlined by Gorbman and others but that they do this in different ways.

Case Study: GoodFellas – a score compiled from popular music

The scores for each of Scorsese's films reflect his eclecticism as a director, some comprising solely of popular songs, others using an orchestral score and popular songs, and others using solely an orchestral score. Scorsese has also worked with a range of composers from Bernard Herrmann and Elmer Bernstein to Howard Shore and Philip Glass and ex-rock musicians Robbie Robertson and Peter Gabriel.[12]

> Music infuses the cinema of Martin Scorsese from the beginning: whether it is the classic rock of *Who's That Knocking at My Door?* (1967) and *Mean Streets* (1973); the twanging bluegrass of *Boxcar Bertha* (1972); the mishmash of pop styles in *Alice Doesn't Live Here Anymore* (1974); or the slinky Bernard Herrmann soundtrack of *Taxi Driver* (1976), music powerfully evokes time, place, even character and action. (Friedman 1999: 89)

The score for *GoodFellas* includes over forty popular songs.[13] An eclectic range of styles is used to indicate period, character growth and mood. The songs are from the various eras depicted in the film and effectively trace the development of popular music in the USA from 1950s Italian-American pop through the classic rock 'n' roll of the 1960s and ending with 1970s punk. Music chronicles the life of the central character, Henry Hill, and plays an important structural role in the film. Much of the story is told through the voice-overs of Henry and his wife, Karen, and music often plays alongside these voice-overs as well as being used both over and under dialogue. However, it is notable that particularly important dialogue does not have music playing. An example of this is when mob member Jimmy Conway tells the young Henry, 'Never rat on your friends and always keep your mouth shut.' Here we will discuss how music is used in the film, particularly its narrative functions and Scorsese's use of musical allusionism.

The song 'Rags to Riches', sung by Tony Bennett, is played over the opening credits of the film. The upbeat, jazzy opening of the song is heard as Henry slams down the car boot and there is the first of many freeze frames used in the film. As the song plays, the images and Henry's voice-over tell the story of his childhood and his desire to be a gangster. The song's title reflects Henry's longing for the glamour and fortune of the gangster lifestyle; this parallels the images as close-ups are shown of shoes, cars, suits and jewellery – all the accoutrements of the gangster lifestyle. The lyrics tell a different story, that 'love is all that ever matters', setting the general mood and stating one of the main themes of the film.

It is generally understood that one of the functions of popular music in film is to denote a particular time period (Smith 1998: 165); Scorsese thinks this is lazy, and wants 'to take advantage of the emotional impact of the music' (quoted in Thompson & Christie 1996: 160).[14] However, this is not to underestimate the need for songs to accurately reflect the extensive time period covered by the film. The rule on *GoodFellas* was to use music which could only have been heard at that time, 'If a scene took place in '73, I could use any music that was current or older' (Thompson & Christie 1996: 161). So there was still a need for the music to accurately reflect the time but Scorsese was also keen for it do much more than that.

Scorsese has been identified by Noel Carroll as one of the filmmakers of the New Hollywood who practices cinematic allusionism, using allusion to film history as an expressive device.[15] Smith relates this to the use of music:

> Allusions to pop music function in much the same manner as the system described by Carroll. On one level, an audience of uninformed viewers may interpret the song as background music pure and simple. As such, they make judgments regarding the overall style and its appropriateness to considerations of setting, character and mood. However, an audience of informed viewers will recognise the song's title, lyrics or performer, and will apply this knowledge to the dramatic context depicted onscreen. In such a way, musical allusion also serves as an expressive device to either comment on the action or suggest the director's attitude toward the characters, settings and themes of the film. (Smith 1998: 167–8)

Smith notes that many of the New Hollywood films, which use cinematic allusionism, have an unmotivated protagonist and whilst this is certainly not the case with Henry what is rarely demonstrated in dialogue, voice-over or images is the emotional side of Henry, or indeed of Karen. It is the music that plays a key role in telling Henry's emotional story and describing his relationship with Karen. At the beginning of the relationship Henry takes Karen on a date, as they get out of the car 'Then He Kissed Me' by The Crystals begins to play nondiegetically. The song continues as Henry takes Karen through a back entrance and through the kitchen into the club, the two are treated like royalty and Henry tips the staff they meet on the way. The whole scene is filmed using one long tracking shot, this continues for the duration of the song as the lyrics tell the story of a developing relationship leading to marriage.

As the relationship progresses Bobby Vinton's 'Roses are Red' is used; this begins to play nondiegetically in a scene where Karen and Henry are on holiday looking blissfully happy. The song then becomes diegetic as Karen and Henry are in a club listening to the song being performed on stage, both the title and lyrics of the song symbolise their developing romance. The Harptones' 'Life is but a Dream' plays over the scene showing Henry and Karen's marriage; during this scene both Henry and Karen again look blissfully happy. This is Karen's introduction to Henry's second family and there are close-ups of the many envelopes containing money which they are given as presents, giving an indication of the importance money (and the lack of it) will play in their lives. The songs during this sequence work on the first level of musical allusionism being appropriate for setting, characterisation and mood as well as operating as an integral part of the narrative.

Smith notes how the second level of musical allusionism, which highlights authorial expressivity by commenting *on* characters rather than speaking from their point of view, differs from the cases just discussed 'in that musical allusionism is used to underline traits which a character may not wish to acknowledge' (1998: 169). In this case the music plays an important part in portraying a side of Henry that Karen does not want to acknowledge as almost immediately problems occur in the marriage. A number of songs operate as a warning to Karen; the first of these is The Shangri-Las' 'Leader of the Pack' with its opening cry of 'Look out, look out, look out, look out'. This is used after Karen rows with her mother about Henry staying out all night; Karen goes to a hostess party at Mickey Conway's and begins to realise how different their lifestyle is as she listens to the other wives talking. This theme is continued with the line 'he sure ain't the way I thought he'd be' from The Crystals' 'He's Sure the Boy I Love' which works as a counterpoint while playing over the scene which leads to the murder of Billy Batts.

Jerry Vale's 'Pretend You Don't See Her' plays at the beginning of Henry's affair with Janice. Henry's voice-over announces that Saturday nights are for the wives and Friday nights are for the girlfriends, as the song plays diegetically, with Vale performing in the club. The emphasis is on the lyrics as the camera pans around the men and their girlfriends sitting at the table watching the performance before closing in on Henry and Janice. The song then becomes nondiegetic as Henry and Janice go home to the apartment he has set her up in. The song continues as the next scene begins with a family get together with Karen and their two children, emphasising the double life Henry is now leading. The title and lyrics of this song can be interpreted in a number of different ways; the title relating to both Karen and Janice ignoring the fact that there is another woman in Henry's life. Whilst for Henry, the line, 'Pretend you don't love her' could be interpreted as him pretending he does not love either Karen or Janice. A further warning sign is given for Karen with the opening line of The Shangri-Las' 'Remember Walking in the Sand'. The lyrics 'whatever happened to the boy I once knew' reflecting Karen's thoughts about her relationship with Henry as his position in the Batts murder becomes more problematic and his relationship with Janice progresses.

FIGURE 3 *GoodFellas* (Martin Scorsese, 1990)

'The Boulevard of Broken Dreams' by Tony Bennett plays briefly after Henry's release from a four-year spell in prison reflecting the shattered dreams of both Henry and Karen. The songs used in the second half of the film continue this theme and reflect the decadent, excessive lifestyle of Henry and Karen as drugs come to play a large part. The use of songs by the Rolling Stones work on a number of levels here. Firstly, they give voice to feelings and attitudes not made explicit by the film's visuals and dialogue; Scorsese has described how they would sometimes put lyrics of songs between lines of dialogue so they commented on action. An example is the use of the Rolling Stones' 'Monkey Man' for the baby drug-smuggling scene with its lyric, 'I'm a flea-bit peanut monkey and all my friends are junkies' (Thompson & Christie 1996: 161). An extract from this track is also used as Henry and Karen are in the car on one of the drug runs. The use of the Rolling Stones also works on a second level, that of musical allusion to the performers. As well as the aforementioned scene, the Stones' 'Gimme Shelter' is played as Sandy, another girlfriend of Henry's, is seen mixing cocaine with a deck of cards. The lyrics also emphasise Henry's need to keep his drug dealing a secret from Paulie and for an informed audience the use of the Rolling Stones alludes to their knowledge of the band's alleged drug-taking exploits and operates as authorial commentary. Scorsese has noted how the music in the film becomes decadent, starkly reflecting Henry's disintegration with drugs (Smith 1990: 30).

This is emphasised with the end sequence of the film featuring Sid Vicious' version of 'My Way'. Shortly before this begins Henry is seen in the courtroom, speaking directly to the camera. The track begins as Henry, now in the Witness Protection Programme, smiles before walking back into his house and slamming the door shut. The song is most well known for Frank Sinatra's rendition and Vicious's delivery is irreverent and mocking, reflecting Henry's nihilistic attitude towards his new life as 'an average nobody'. The lyrics also speak for Henry, he did it his way, and did the very thing he was told not to do by Jimmy Conway early in the film – he ratted on his friends and did not keep his mouth shut. Henry's behaviour in the courtroom, along with the use of this version of 'My Way' can be interpreted as a somewhat playful ending to the film, which undercuts its serious tone.

Whilst much of this discussion has focused on the importance of lyrics it should be noted that the lyrics of many of the songs used in the film are not always heard clearly, and of equal importance is the melody, mood and tone of the music. Scorsese has said, 'The music was mainly chosen for the rhythm and emotion of each scene' (Thompson & Christie 1996: 161). It is also clear that a great deal of thought went into the choice of songs and that they were an integral part of the script rather than being added in post-production. Scorsese describes trying ten different songs for the scene where Jimmy is planning to kill Morrie Kessler, eventually using Cream's 'Sunshine of Your Love',

> I used that song for the scene when Jimmy is at the bar ... and the camera moves into his face very slowly ... we found his eyes were just perfect with that shot at high speed, and it gave a real sense of danger and sexuality. (Ibid.)

This score of popular songs still fulfills many of the functions of the classical score; both melody and lyrics are used to signify emotion, whilst song titles and lyrics often operate as a narrative cue. *GoodFellas* also provides another counter-example to Smith's idea that a compilation score is much less likely to be used as an element of structural and rhythmic continuity. Despite the fact that the majority of the songs are played only once so there are no themes, the songs themselves provide continuity by providing a soundtrack and a structure to Henry's life story. In addition the use of musical allusionism gives added meaning to the film for both an informed and an uninformed audience.

It is clear from the examples used here that a wide range of music – both classical and popular – can fulfill the functions of film music as outlined earlier in this chapter; the examples used also demonstrate the affective power of both diegetic and nondiegetic music. Contemporary films are using an increasing range of music, which serves different purposes and also works on different levels for different audiences.

3   POPULAR MUSIC IN FILM: A CASE STUDY – MAGNOLIA

Popular music is the only cultural reference we hold in common
anymore. (Allison Anders in Romney & Wootton 1995: 119)

The influence of popular music on film has been the topic of much discussion, and is a recurring theme throughout this book. As demonstrated in
chapter one, this is not a new phenomenon however; since the late 1960s
it has become much more noticeable. There have been many examples
of films named after pop songs but there are still few examples of pop
songs influencing the writing of film scripts.[1] This chapter discusses the
way in which popular songs have influenced *The Graduate* (1967), *McCabe
and Mrs Miller* (1971) and *Singles* (1992). Following this is a detailed case
study of *Magnolia* (1999), directed by Paul Thomas Anderson, examining
the influence of popular music on the film and also considering the textual
and commercial functions of the music.

There is now a whole generation of filmmakers who have grown up
with popular music. Many contemporary filmmakers have commented
on the importance of music in the filmmaking process: 'You can make an
argument that music is the soul of the film' (Alan Rudolph in Romney and
Wootton 1995: 119); 'I think I decided to be a filmmaker the moment that I
put a piece of music to film' (Penelope Spheeris in Romney & Wootton 1995:
122); 'My films are all super music-influenced. The soul of them comes
from music. When I write my scripts I listen to music. [It's] my major source
of inspiration' (Greg Araki in Gdula 1999: 72).

Directors such as Martin Scorsese, Quentin Tarantino and Paul Thomas
Anderson select songs for use in their films during script development and

in some cases these are directly written into the screenplay. Tarantino has discussed how he tries to find the right song for the opening credit sequence before he writes the script: 'I'd hear music and I would imagine a scene for it' (Tarantino in Romney & Wootton 1995: 130).

The Graduate was extremely influential in its use of popular music as score. The film is a comedy about an innocent graduate who finds himself alienated and is exploited and seduced by the mother of one of his friends. It has been described as the first major Hollywood hit to feature a score by a rock star (Knobloch 1997: 61).[2] Simon and Garfunkel were popular musicians at the time the movie was filmed and the music featured in the film is mainly pre-recorded songs, which were in wide circulation prior to the release of the film. Paul Simon wrote the songs but recording credits are shared with Art Garfunkel. It appears that with this film the practice of working with a *'temp score'** dramatically affected the use of music in the final film.[3] Whilst Simon had been commissioned to write the score, director Mike Nichols was using existing material where the score was supposed to be: 'He decided that that material was absolutely appropriate, so the only new song that made it in there was "Mrs. Robinson"' (Simon in Knobloch 1997: 61).

Interestingly, Simon and Garfunkel's music is mainly presented non-diegetically and in isolation from other sounds in the film, whereas the *incidental music** composed by jazz musician Dave Grusin is used diegetically. Throughout the film the songs bring out important character traits of Benjamin. The lyrics of the two main songs used, 'Sounds of Silence' and 'Scarboro' Fair' enhance the film's moods and themes. 'Sounds of Silence' is used over the opening credits of the film where its haunting lyrics reinforce Benjamin's alienation from his surroundings in the airport. The same song is used later in the film in a montage scene, which begins with Benjamin floating on a pool mattress and ends with him in bed with Mrs Robinson; during this scene it functions as a motif for his withdrawal. Elsewhere, the song 'Scarboro' Fair' acts as an interior monologue for Benjamin. As well as using the actual songs, during the last third of the film the use of music changes and Nichols uses 'cues' derived from Simon's songs. As Susan Knobloch notes:

> The choice of Paul Simon to score *The Graduate* established a rela-
> tionship between score and film – based upon the idea of something
> important to the images existing independently of them. (1997: 71)

Director Robert Altman uses music in an unusual manner in his films.[4] He has also set up a model of filmmaking and narrative exposition whose influence can be felt in Anderson's *Magnolia*, with multiple characters and stories centered around a particular event, space or institution. *McCabe and Mrs Miller* features three songs by singer-songwriter Leonard Cohen, 'The Stranger Song', 'Sisters of Mercy' and 'Winter Lady'. As with *The Graduate*, the songs were pre-recorded and in circulation prior to the release of the film, having been released in 1968 on Cohen's first album, *Songs of Leonard Cohen*. In this case Cohen's songs were influential in the editing process; Cohen has said that Altman actually built the film around his music. Altman had listened to Cohen's music in an earlier period and then found it resurfacing in his head whilst vacationing after the wrap of *McCabe and Mrs Miller*. Altman called Cohen to ask if his music could be used; Cohen had just seen Altman's previous film, *Brewster McCloud* (1970), which he thought was extraordinary, and told Altman he could 'use any music of mine' (Cohen quoted in Kubernik & Pierce 1975).[5]

The film is a western which tells the story of a businessman, McCabe and his fortunes when he arrives in a small mining town, and meets Mrs Miller, the woman who helps his business and subsequently falls in love

FIGURE 4 *The Graduate* (Mike Nichols, 1967)

with him. The songs are very different to the music usually used in westerns, but then this is no ordinary western; the film has been described as an 'anti-western'. Altman's emphasis is on the ambience and atmosphere; the songs are integral to the mood of the film and work to connect the storyline, at times synchronising with the images or story and at other times working as a counterpoint.

Director Cameron Crowe is an ex-rock journalist who has always featured music heavily in his films. On being asked how music informs his conception of a film Crowe replied, 'It starts with the music. Always. I hear the movie before I can ever write it' (Crowe in Tobias 2000). *Singles* tracks the relationships of six Seattle singles in their early to mid-twenties whose lives are spent in and around the Seattle music scene; it has been described as 'a movie built upwards from a collection of songs by bands' (Kermode 1995: 12). Music is used as a dramatic theme in the film and figures prominently; members of Pearl Jam play Matt Dillon's band mates in the fictional group Citizen Dick, there are also live performances from Soundgarden and Alice in Chains. The film itself is structured like an album, every ten minutes or so a title card appears on the screen, this effectively divides the film into sections analogous to tracks or singles on an album.

Crowe commissioned Paul Westerberg, formerly a member of seminal rock band The Replacements, to write a special song for the film. The result was 'Dyslexic Heart'[6] and Crowe was so pleased with this that he commissioned another song, 'Waiting for Somebody'. Crowe then wanted to incorporate the themes of these two songs into the score of the film and this led to Westerberg writing the score for the film, the themes being based on the two songs. In addition to this new songs were written by Smashing Pumpkins, Soundgarden, Screaming Trees, Alice in Chains and Pearl Jam and the soundtrack also included oldies from Mother Love Bone and Seattle-born Jimi Hendrix.[7]

In each of the aforementioned films popular music has played a key role and this is developed even further in Anderson's *Magnolia*.

Magnolia – a case study

> I sat down to write an adaptation of Aimee Mann songs. Like one would adapt a book for the screen, I had the concept of adapting Aimee's songs into a screenplay. (Anderson 1999)

Magnolia is written, directed and produced by Paul Thomas Anderson, and is his third feature film following *Hard Eight* (1996) and *Boogie Nights* (1997).[8] The film has twelve main characters whose lives intersect in nine intertwined stories over the course of one day in California's San Fernando Valley. As the film progresses, the connections between the characters become apparent; even those characters that are not connected in a physical way, are connected symbolically as they deal with the need for love. Redemption through love is a specific motif throughout the film and at several points in the film characters are shown as having love to give, but not knowing how to show it.

In a similar way to the techniques used by Nichols in *The Graduate* and Altman in *McCabe and Mrs Miller*, Anderson uses the songs of one main artist to anchor the film with the nine storylines set mainly to a soundtrack of songs by singer-songwriter Aimee Mann. The film also includes two songs by Supertramp ('Goodbye Stranger' and 'Logical Song'), 'Dreams' by Gabrielle, and an orchestral score composed by Jon Brion. In the three-hour film Brion's score plays for over one hour in total whereas Mann's songs are featured for only one-third of that time; however, it is Mann's songs that provide the framework for the film and that will be discussed here. The majority of Mann's songs featured in the film were released for the first time on the soundtrack album. The two exceptions to this being 'Wise Up', which had previously appeared on the CD soundtrack of *Jerry Maguire* (1996), and her cover of Nilsson's 'One', previously recorded for a Nilsson tribute anthology. Two songs, 'Save Me' and 'You Do' were written specifically for the film, the others being songs Mann was working on for her next album.

Anderson describes himself as being a fan first and friend second of Aimee Mann's (Anderson 2003). He was listening to her music at the same time he was starting to write the script for *Magnolia*: 'Everything she seemed to be thinking were things that I was thinking' (Anderson 1999). Anderson was particularly inspired by the lyrics to one song, 'Deathly', taking the opening line from the song and writing backwards from that:

> Now that I've met you
> Would you object to
> Never seeing each other again

Anderson has discussed how this song 'equals the story of Claudia. It equals the heart and soul of *Magnolia*. All stories for the movie were written branching off from Claudia, so one could do the math and realise that all stories come from Aimee's brain, not mine' (Anderson 1999). Mann's songs have dramatic functions in the film and commercial functions outside of the film, both of which will be discussed here. Firstly, the textual use of popular music in *Magnolia* will be discussed using arguments put forward by Claudia Gorbman and Jeff Smith as outlined in chapter two. Four scenes from the film will be used in order to analyse the role that Mann's songs play in the narrative, characterisation and themes of the film. Using the chapter titles from the DVD release of *Magnolia*, the scenes to be discussed are; firstly, the opening credits sequence, 'One'; secondly, 'Momentum'; thirdly 'Wise Up'; and fourthly, 'Save Me'. There will also be a brief discussion of the other songs used in the film. Secondly, the commercial functions of the popular music will be discussed examining the marketing of the film and the impact on Mann's career.

There is always a strong narrative drive to Mann's songs, as well as a sense of romantic disappointment, which works perfectly with the feelings of characters in the film. Music is central to the storyline of *Magnolia*, as it sets the tone and has a unique way of advancing plot, each song moving the story forward. The working process was symbiotic, and Mann was brought in as the script developed:

> I would read some of the script and play some music and fit it in thematically. There were a couple of songs that were written that way back and forth. (Mann in Houlihan 2000)

'One'

After the Prologue the opening credits appear with Mann's cover of Nilsson's 'One' playing, this is a long sequence with the song extended from the CD version of just under three minutes to six and a half minutes.[9] The song sets the stage for this ensemble film where everyone is very much alone and the lyrics relate directly to the themes of film.

> One is the loneliest number
> That you'll ever do
> Two can be as bad as one,
> it's the loneliest number
> since the number one

During this section the audience is introduced to eleven of the main characters and to the narrative of the film. Frank Mackey (Tom Cruise), the television guru of female seduction; Claudia Wilson Gator (Melora Walters), the cocaine-addicted daughter of television presenter Jimmy Gator (Philip Baker Hall) who is dying from cancer, and his wife Rose (Melinda Dillon); child-genius-turned-quiz-show-star Stanley Spector (Jeremy Blackman) and his father Rick (Michael Bowen); 1960s quiz-show star, Donnie Smith (William H. Macy); Phil Parma (Philip Seymour Hoffman), nurse to dying television producer Earl Partridge (Jason Robards), whose last wish is to communicate with his lost son; Earl's wife, Linda Partridge (Julianne Moore); and compassionate police officer Jim Kurring (John C. Reilly) who is looking for love.

During most of this section the music plays alongside dialogue and sound effects; at one point a short section of Gabrielle's 'Dreams' is also heard. Although the audience do not realise it at the time, all of these characters lives will be connected and one of the major themes of the film – that of family relationships – is established here. Mann's song in this scene follows the conventions of opening credits music as outlined by Gorbman:

> It identifies the genre ... and it sets a general mood ... Further it often states one or more themes to be heard later accompanying the story ... Finally, opening-title music signals that the story is about to begin. (1987: 82)

'Momentum'

The song 'Momentum' plays diegetically throughout the scene where police officer Jim Curring is called to Claudia's apartment.[10] He has been called as she is playing her music too loud, and the volume increases as Claudia in seen in her apartment. The lyrics of the song are of direct relevance to the character of Claudia and her emotions, signifying her feeling that life is passing her by; her pessimism about the future; and also her abuse by, and subsequent problems with, her father:

> I can't admit that maybe the past was bad
> And so, for the sake of momentum
> I'm condemning the future to death
> So it can match the past

As Jim is seen outside Claudia's apartment door, the music increases in volume again and is blasting as she opens the door. The emphasis here is on the audible quality of the music, which works in opposition to Gorbman's theory of 'inaudibility'. The music is very much part of the diegesis and serves a dual narrative purpose – that of introducing Claudia and Jim to each other, whilst the lyrics serve the purpose of giving an insight into Claudia's emotions.

'Wise Up'

The section of the film that uses Mann's song 'Wise Up' is perhaps the most interesting with regard to the use of the music. During this montage section Anderson has nine of the main characters sing along with Mann's vocals. With the exception of Phil and Earl, each of the characters is seen alone when singing. The lyrics can be related to the feelings of each individual character as well as operating to unify the characters and the intertwined storylines. The opening chords of the song are heard as Claudia is seen sitting alone in her apartment, Mann is then heard singing the opening lines. The song begins softly, then gets a bit louder and Claudia starts to sing along:

> It's not
> What you thought
> When you first began it
> You got
> What you want
> Now you can hardly stand it, though
> By now you know
> It's not going to stop

As the song continues each of the principle characters are seen half-singing along, although Mann's vocal is heard throughout. A male voice is heard and Jim is sitting on the bed ready to go out, he also sings along to the song:

> It's not going to stop
> It's not going to stop
> 'Til you wise up

Jimmy is sitting in his office and sings:

> You're sure
> There's a cure
> And you have finally found it

Then Donnie sings in his apartment:

> You think
> One drink
> Will shrink you
> 'Til you're underground
> And living down
> But it's not going to stop

Then at Earl's house, first Phil is seen holding back his tears and singing as he sits next to Earl, before Earl joins in:

> It's not going to stop
> It's not going to stop
> 'Til you wise up

Then Linda is seen in her car, she also starts to sing along:

> Prepare a list of what you need
> Before you sign away the deed
> 'Cause it's not going to stop

A male voice is then heard singing; this is Frank, also in his car:

> It's not going to stop
> No, it's not going to stop
> 'Til you wise up
> No, it's not going to stop
> 'Til you wise up
> No it's not going to stop

Finally, Stanley is seen singing in the school library:

So just give up

The lines sung by many of the characters signify their emotional feelings; for example Jimmy sings the lines about finding a cure which can be related to his illness and also to his problem relationship with Claudia. Donnie sings the line about drinking linked to the key scenes in the bar when his inner feelings are revealed; Linda sings the line about signing away the deed that can be related to Earl's will; and Stanley's final line 'So just give up' emphasises his despondency.

The lyrics of the song seem to fit so perfectly it is hard to believe that Mann did not write this specifically for the film. Anderson said that on one level he wanted, 'to play into the cliché of how we see movie characters singing along with Motown'; on the other level, he wanted one moment that would unite *Magnolia*'s vast array of disparate plots and unrelated characters, and music was the best way to do it (Borrelli 2000). It is interesting that he chose one of Mann's songs to unify the plots and characters rather than Brion's orchestral score. Kathryn Kalinak has argued that 'the formal autonomy of popular music can sometimes lessen its chances of being used to maintain structural unity or continuity' (1992: 187) which is usually done through the use of leitmotifs. This example shows that popular music can be used to maintain continuity and unity, as also proved by Lauren Anderson in her analysis of *Sliding Doors* and discussed in chapter two.

It is not immediately clear that the 'Wise Up' sequence is going to be a full musical number:

I thought the best way to do that sequence was to have it creep up on you ... By the time it cuts to Philip Baker Hall, you've been hoodwinked into a musical number! (Anderson in Willman 2000: 67)

This sequence also works on the level of authorial expressivity. Smith discusses instances where an element of authorial expressivity is used to comment on characters rather than speaking from their point of view, underlining traits a character may not wish to acknowledge (1998: 169). 'Wise Up' works on both levels here as it expresses each individual characters' point of view and is also a comment on each one of the characters who is going through their own personal crisis, and coming to the realisation that the source of their disaffection is partly within themselves and that they can have some control over this. The repetition of the lyric 'It's not going to stop/'Til you wise up' reinforces this, emphasising that they need to try and take control of their lives.

Gorbman has suggested that in scenes from dramatic films where a character sings a song, the action necessarily freezes for the duration of the song. Anderson is aware of the problems of having characters break into song in contemporary films:

> Have one character break into song today and you risk torpedoing your movie ... The modern audience isn't prepared to selectively suspend their disbelief and drift from realism to fantasy without raising their eyebrows. (Anderson in Borrelli 2000)

The risk taken by Anderson pays off here. The lyrics of 'Wise Up' are part of the narrative and the action does not freeze for the duration of the song. Music is not subordinated to dialogue – it *is* the dialogue and functions as an expression of different characters' points of view. This is also an experience the audience can relate to as people often sing along to songs when expressing emotions of either happiness or sadness.

'Save Me'

'Save Me' is one of the two songs Mann wrote especially for *Magnolia*; it is used at the end of the film and continues over some of the end credits. As with 'One' this is extended from the CD version of four and a half minutes to eight minutes. This scene emphasises the beginning of the relationship between Claudia and Jim; Claudia is seen sitting up in bed, she is staring into space and looks tearful. As she looks up she sees someone enter the room and a male voice is heard saying, 'I just wanted to come here'. It becomes clear this is Jim and he then sits down on the edge of the bed and the two of them talk. At this point the volume of the dialogue is so low it is virtually impossible to hear what is being said; instead the lyrics of the song speak not only for Claudia but also for many of the other characters who all want to be saved in some way. The song begins hesitatingly:

> But can you save me
> Come on and save me
> If you could save me

From the ranks
Of the freaks who suspect
They could never love anyone

The lyrics then connote the realisation that Claudia feels she has found a soul mate, someone who knows how she feels, 'Cause I can tell/You know what it's like'. As the song ends it reflects Claudia's growing confidence that she will be saved, and her sense of surprise at finding someone like Jim:

You struck me dumb
Like radium
Like Peter Pan
Or Superman
You will come
To save me

The last shot of the film shows Claudia looking into the camera and smiling, the lyrics signifying the sense of hope and optimism she feels about meeting Jim.

'Deathly'

Whilst the song 'Deathly' is not included in the film it is featured on the soundtrack album and, as mentioned previously, the lyrics very much tell Claudia's story. As well as the aforementioned opening lyric being used as dialogue, another lyric is also used as Claudia says to Jim, 'I've got troubles'. The chorus of this song strongly reflects Claudia's feelings once she has met Jim, warning against the possible impact of 'one act of kindness':

So don't work your stuff
Because I've got troubles enough
No, don't pick on me
When one act of kindness could be
Deathly, Deathly
Definitely

Chapter two discussed the importance of lyrics when songs are used in film; Smith has suggested that the lyrics of popular music offer a kind of 'double-edged sword, carrying a potential for distraction but also "speaking for" characters or commenting on the film's action (1998: 166). Whilst Gorbman asks 'Has it become "normal" to listen to a rock song with lyrics at the same time as we follow a story?' (1987: 163). Mann has said that Anderson 'understands that the lyrics substitute for narration or dialogue. People will pay attention to words set to music, especially in a movie where they're a captive audience' (Anon. 2000).

The lyrics to Mann's songs are integral to the story in *Magnolia* so images, music and dialogue work together. The songs speak for the characters and also comment on the film's actions, this is also the case with the three songs by other artists used in the film, which we shall consider next.

The song 'Dreams' by Gabrielle is associated with the character of Donnie Smith throughout the film and acts as a theme for his character. Short extracts of 'Dreams' are used seven times in the film, always diegetically and always associated with Donnie in his car.

> Dreams can come true
> Look at me babe if I'm with you
> You know you've gotta have hope
> You know you've got to be strong

This song also works to maintain a sense of continuity with the character of Donnie, despite the fact that only very brief extracts are heard at any one time. Lauren Anderson has noted how 'even when only a brief snatch of a popular song is heard in a film, it automatically alludes to the presence of the rest of the song as a separate entity existing outside the soundtrack' (2003: 170).

It is this structural independence that can prevent pop songs being used for some of the 'classical' film music functions and can sometimes lessen its chances of being used to maintain structural unity or continuity. However through its repetition, 'Dreams' works as a leitmotif to structurally unify the plot and its episodic narrative and becomes associated with Donnie's feelings.

The two Supertramp songs featured on the soundtrack CD are also used in connection with the character of Donnie, and appear at key scenes in the film during which the audience learns a great deal about Donnie's thoughts and feelings. The first Supertramp song, 'Goodbye Stranger', is heard almost in full as Donnie first walks into the bar after having been fired from his job:

> And I will go on shining
> Shining like brand new
> I'll never look behind me
> My troubles will be few

> Goodbye stranger it's been nice
> Hope you find your paradise
> Tried to see your point of view
> Hope your dreams will all come true

The last line also makes a connection with 'Dreams'. The second Supertramp song, 'Logical Song', is again heard as Donnie is in the bar and is again played almost in full. The lyrics of this song can be related to Donnie's success as a child and the identity crisis he finds himself in as an adult searching for love:

> When I was young, it seemed that life was so wonderful,
> a miracle, oh it was beautiful, magical.

During this scene Donnie questions his own identity and knowledge as it becomes clear that his parents took the money he won as a child genius on *What do Kids Know?* The significance of 'Dreams' is again reiterated as Donnie says, 'I'll make my dreams come true, you'll see', signifying his hope for the future.

The commercial functions of popular music in Magnolia

The commercial uses of the soundtrack to *Magnolia* are interesting; firstly, in terms of the marketing of the film and how this differs from the usual commercial use of a soundtrack album; and secondly, how this relates to the career of Aimee Mann. As is now common practice, there were two CD soundtrack releases, one of the orchestral score and one of the songs. The first to be released was titled 'Music from the motion picture' with 'Songs by Aimee Mann' stated on the CD cover; this features nine songs performed by Aimee Mann, two songs by Supertramp, and the *Magnolia* theme by Jon

Brion.[11] The second CD soundtrack release was the 'Original Motion Picture Score' composed by Jon Brion, released three months afterwards. It is the first CD, of Aimee Mann songs, that will be discussed here.

The established formula for a film soundtrack in Hollywood is that the film is made, then either high-profile bands are asked to contribute songs or songs are selected for the film, the songs are put onto a CD and the CD is sold to make as much money as possible. In many cases, not all of the songs appearing in the film will appear on the soundtrack CD; in addition, the soundtrack CD sometimes includes songs not featured in the film. (This is discussed in further detail in chapter five.) *Magnolia* is an exception, the major difference here being that not only were some of Mann's songs written especially for the film but they also played an integral part in the development of the script. The process of writing was a collaborative one between Mann and Anderson, and the music was not added as an afterthought.

Artists usually have little or no say in how their music is used in a film; it may not be used at all or may be used for only a few seconds. Mann has commented on the use of her music in films and the pressure put on directors:[12]

> I've had songs here and there on soundtracks, but I've never had my songs utilised in such an integral way. I don't think a lot of directors do that anyway. Mostly, there's pressure on directors to make a deal with the record company and use whatever acts the record company is trying to push in the movie and on the soundtrack. (Mann in Morse 1999)[13]

This raises interesting points about creative control and the role of the director and the studio in deciding on film music, issues which are discussed in chapter five. Danny Bramson, Reprise Records' Senior Vice President of soundtrack development and the *Magnolia* soundtrack's executive producer,[14] described Anderson as being, 'one of the rare filmmakers who truly loves music and instinctively knows how to integrate it – rather than force it in to use it as a marketing tool' (Bramson in Bessman 1999). Throughout the history of film there are examples of directors who pay great attention to the inclusion of music in their films and do indeed integrate it (as discussed in the beginning of this chapter and also in chapter one). It often appears to be the case that it is the film company, rather than the director, who is keen to include music purely as a marketing tool.

However, the marketing of this soundtrack was still important. There is undeniably a market there for Aimee Mann songs and the story behind the soundtrack became part of the marketing campaign. Peter Rauh, Warner Bros. Marketing Vice President, described how this 'artist-driven soundtrack', gives the record a duality atypical of soundtrack marketing – working almost as the new Aimee Mann album, as well as a film soundtrack (Bessman 1999).

The music video is usually a major part of a marketing campaign being used as a promotional device on MTV and other forums for promotion. The video for the single release of 'Save Me' is also different to the usual music video from a film which incorporates footage from the film intercut with footage of the artist performing. The video was directed by Anderson and was shot at the same time as the film. It features Mann in a scene with each of the major actors in the film, sometimes singing to them, at other times singing direct to camera. Rauh describes how Anderson would shoot scenes with the actors in character and then stop and replace them with Mann and reshoot it as a piece of the video. 'So there will be a scene in the movie with Julianne Moore and the same scene in the video with Mann singing, rather than just intercutting film footage into the video' (Bessman 1999).

Aimee Mann's career in the music industry and contractual problems with various record companies has been well documented. During the 1980s Mann was the lead singer and songwriter in Boston based band Til Tuesday who released three critically acclaimed albums. In the late 1980s she spent three years trying to get out of her contract with Epic Records. She then released two solo albums which were again critically acclaimed; however, further contractual problems with Geffen Records followed and Mann went on to release her third solo album, *Bachelor No. 2*, on her own label. Mann had always maintained that a record company's job is marketing: 'I've always maintained that if people could just hear my records, maybe some of them would buy it' (Anon. 2000). In terms of the impact of *Magnolia*'s success on her own career Mann has said:

> Having music in a popular film does the job that the record company doesn't always do. People send fan mail to my website saying that they saw *Magnolia*, thought the music was great, found out who I was and bought the record. (Mann in Levitan 2000)

FIGURE 5 Music video for 'Save Me', with Melora Walters ('Claudia Wilson Gator') and Aimee Mann (right)

Whilst not hugely successful Mann is an artist with a following of dedicated fans, and there is a definite audience for her work. The release of the soundtrack of *Magnolia* came almost five years after her previous release and was seen by many as a new Aimee Mann album which fans would buy regardless of the film. Mann's songs on *Magnolia* were again critically acclaimed and brought her work to a much wider audience than previously. There was also official recognition with 'Save Me' being nominated for Best Music, Song at the Oscars; Best Original Song at the Golden Globes; and Best Song written for a Motion Picture at the Grammy's.[15] Mann's songs also played a prominent role in the trailers and television spots advertising the film.

To return to the overall analysis, Smith's discussion of musical allusionism, as outlined in chapter two, seems particularly significant with regard to Mann's songs in *Magnolia*. Firstly, the use of musical allusionism to 'speak' for character, and secondly, the use of music to reinforce narrative or generic themes (1998: 168). As many of Mann's songs were new to the soundtrack, I would suggest that in this case musical allusionism works in relation to Mann as a performer. To anyone who is familiar with Mann's previous work it is clear that the character of Claudia and her story is also the character and story in many of Mann's songs – one of the central themes of *Magnolia,* the search for love, is a constant theme in Mann's work.

In many ways the popular songs in *Magnolia* function in the same way as a classic orchestral score. They serve the narrative, they signify emotion and are used to sustain structural unity. However, they challenge Gorbman's theory by their audibility; indeed rather than being subordinated to the dialogue at times they function as dialogue. The songs also fulfill the functions of popular music in film as outlined by Smith. The lyrics give voice to feelings and attitudes not made explicit by the visuals and dialogue, they highlight the element of authorial expressivity, they work as musical allusionism to speak for characters; it could also be said that Mann's songs work to denote a particular period of time.[16] Anderson has chosen songs that work well with the dialogue and create narrative continuity to the film as well as giving an insight into characters' emotions and feelings. Anderson has often said that what Simon and Garfunkel's songs were to *The Graduate*, Mann's songs are to *Magnolia* – 'part of the inseparable whole' (Anderson in Wilonsky 1999).

Whilst it is clear that the music was included as an integral part of the narrative and not as a pure marketing tool it is also clear that marketing of the soundtrack was important. The concept of synergy plays a vital role here; *Magnolia* the film was released by New Line, part of the major entertainment conglomerate AOL Time Warner, and both of the CD soundtracks were released by Reprise Records, part of the same group. It is the music video for Mann's 'Save Me' that is of perhaps the most importance here. The video sees the artist whose songs inspired the screenplay, and play an integral part in the film, appear on the film set with each of the main characters in a promotional video for a song from the film. She is seen sitting next to Claudia in her apartment, in the bar with Donnie, as a contestant on the set of *What do Kids Know?* with Stanley, and in the back of Jim's police car. This demonstrates the full impact of the symbiotic relationship between film and popular music.

The examples given in this chapter demonstrate the increasing influence of popular music on the working practices of contemporary directors who have fully integrated popular songs into the narrative of their films.

4   POPULAR MUSICIANS AS FILM COMPOSERS

This chapter examines the increasing numbers of pop stars and rock musicians who have composed music for film. It is necessary first to clarify the terms being used and what will be included in this chapter. The term popular (pop) musician will be used to incorporate musicians from the rock, pop, jazz and dance worlds all of whom have become established through their career in the popular music industry before moving into composing for film. Whilst many pop musicians have contributed music to films the emphasis here is on those instances where they have composed either music or songs especially for film. This chapter will, firstly, chronicle the involvement of pop musicians composing for film; secondly, examine the possible reasons for this practice from the perspectives of the industry and also of the musicians themselves; and thirdly, will consider how this applies to Damon Albarn, a member of the band Blur who has recently moved into composing for film.

As discussed in previous chapters, there has always been a close relationship between popular music and film. Since the 1950s there have been an increasing number of popular musicians acting in films; the music industry has also been used as a setting for films; there have been rockumentaries; films named after songs; bands naming themselves and their releases after films; and an increasing use of pop music in film used both diegetically and, more importantly, nondiegetically.[1] Some artists showed the influence of film in other ways, in 1978 the new wave band Magazine recorded the theme from *Goldfinger*, Barry Adamson of the band began his solo career with a cover of Elmer Bernstein's 'The Man with the Golden Arm' in 1988 and went on to compose music for non-existent films before composing for actual films.[2]

A chronicle of popular musicians composing for film

Whilst little has been written about popular musicians composing for film[3] articles about the use of pop music in films tend to focus on the American films *The Graduate* (1967) and *Easy Rider* (1969). *The Graduate* is of particular relevance here with its score comprised of songs by Simon and Garfunkel; however prior to this a number of jazz musicians had written film scores. Miles Davis for *Lift to the Scaffold* (Louis Malle, 1958), Duke Ellington for *Anatomy of a Murder* (Otto Preminger, 1959) and Quincy Jones for *The Pawnbroker* (Sidney Lumet, 1964). All three went on to compose more film scores.

In the 1960s there were also a number of British films featuring music composed by popular musicians. *Catch Us If You Can* (John Boorman, 1965), featuring the Dave Clark Five, had a jazz-inflected score provided by the band as well as featuring their songs nondiegetically. *Here We Go Round the Mulberry Bush* (Clive Donner, 1967) had a score provided by the Spencer Davis Group and Traffic. The film version of *Up the Junction* (Peter Collinson, 1967) used a score written and performed by Manfred Mann, and also uses pop songs nondiegetically.[4] Paul McCartney composed the score for *The Family Way* (Roy Boulting, 1966); his music was adapted and orchestrated by Beatles' producer George Martin.[5] Another member of the Beatles, George Harrison, wrote the score for *Wonderwall* (Joe Massot, 1968).

The 1970s saw a definite move from the pop music world into film scoring; this period also saw a crossover between film music and pop music. David Toop notes how, from the late 1960s, experimentation and fragmentation became endemic in popular music: 'From psychedelia onwards, the adventurous end of rock and pop evolved into a kind of film music without film' (1995: 79). Film scoring offered further opportunities for experimentation and bands such as Pink Floyd and Tangerine Dream moved into composing film soundtracks. Pink Floyd scored *More* (Barbet Schroeder, 1969); *Zabriskie Point* (Michaelangelo Antonioni, 1970), with Jerry Garcia of the Grateful Dead; and *La Vallée* (Barbet Schroeder, 1972). Tangerine Dream scored *The Wages of Fear* (aka *Sorcerer*, Henri-Georges Clouzot, 1977).[6]

Isaac Hayes won an Academy Award for his mainly instrumental score for *Shaft* (1971) and went on to score *Truck Turner* (Jonathan Kaplan, 1974) and *Three Tough Guys* (Duccio Tessari, 1974). Hayes had experimented with his own solo material and Toop suggests that film scoring was the next step for him; he also knew how to 'cater for the blaxploitation target audience of black youth' (1995: 78). Smith suggests that the success of Isaac Hayes' score for *Shaft*,

> served as both a signal of industry change and a harbinger of things to come ... Hayes' emergence clearly suggests the industry's growing acceptance of pop, funk, soul and rock musicians as legitimate scorers. (1998: 67)

The 1980s saw a continued increase in the use of pop musicians as film composers. Nile Rodgers composed scores for *Coming to America* (John Landis, 1988) and *Earth Girls are Easy* (Julien Temple, 1988); Ry Cooder for *Paris, Texas* (Wim Wenders, 1984) and a series of Walter Hill films;[7] and Tom Waits for *One From the Heart* (Francis Ford Coppola, 1982). Ex-Police frontman Sting played the lead role in *Brimstone and Treacle* (Richard Loncraine, 1982) and although Michael Nyman is credited with additional music, the film is almost entirely scored by the Police. Both Sting and Stewart Copeland of the band went on to compose both orchestral scores and songs for film.

A number of popular musicians from once popular bands also moved into composing for film in the 1980s. Eric Clapton had been a member of the Yardbirds in the early 1960s before forming Cream in 1966, he then joined Derek and the Dominoes in 1970, before pursuing a successful solo career. Clapton had worked on Scorsese's *Mean Streets* in 1973 and in the 1980s and 1990s collaborated with composer Michael Kamen on all of the *Lethal Weapon* films (Richard Donner, 1987; 1989; 1992; 1998), as well as scoring *Rush* (Lili Fini Zanuck, 1991) and *Nil By Mouth* (Gary Oldman, 1997) amongst others. Mark Knopfler was the frontman for Dire Straits who achieved huge success in the 1980s. Knopfler moved into scoring for film at the height of Dire Straits popularity, his score for *Local Hero* (Bill Forsyth, 1983) bringing together, 'the traditional effects of musical underscores for films with the retention of his individual musical identity' (Donnelly 2001b: 102). Knopfler also composed scores for *Cal* (Pat O'Connor, 1984), *Comfort and Joy* (Bill Forsyth, 1984), and *Last Exit to Brooklyn* (Uli Edel, 1989). Peter Gabriel was lead singer of art rock band Genesis in the 1970s before moving on to a solo career; he has composed scores for *Birdy* (Alan Parker, 1984), *The Last Temptation of Christ* (Martin Scorsese, 1988), *Strange Days*

(Kathryn Bigelow, 1995),[8] *Rabbit-Proof Fence* (Phillip Noyce, 2002) and *Gangs of New York* (Martin Scorsese, 2002). Each of these artists have made a career out of film scoring rather than it being a one-off diversion; in addition all still maintain their career as pop musician.

Japanese musician Ryuichi Sakamoto is most well known as a member of the Yellow Magic Orchestra, an influential techno-pop trio in the late 1970s and early 1980s. Sakamoto accepted an acting role in *Merry Christmas, Mr Lawrence* (Nagisa Oshima, 1983), on the condition that he could compose the score; the same thing happened with *The Last Emperor* (Bernardo Bertolluci, 1987) for which his score won an Academy Award. Sakamoto has gone on to become one of the most successful popular musicians in scoring for mainstream films. The late Joe Strummer, ex-Clash frontman, worked with director Alex Cox on three films, *Sid and Nancy* (1986), *Straight to Hell* (1987) and *Walker* (1987). Strummer's record company contract meant he could only be credited for two songs on *Sid and Nancy*, although he did write and perform more. Strummer took on acting roles in *Straight to Hell* and *Walker* and also composed the score for *Walker*. Meanwhile ex-Band member Robbie Robertson developed a working relationship with Scorsese working as music producer/consultant on a number of films including *Raging Bull* (1980), *Casino* (1995) and *Gangs of New York* (2002). Robertson also composed the score for Scorsese's *The Color of Money* (1986), Barry Levinson's *Jimmy Hollywood* (1994) and Oliver Stone's *Any Given Sunday* (1999).

Whilst the 1980s saw a number of established popular musicians move into the field of film scoring, the 1990s saw an emphasis on independent artists composing for independent film. Examples include J. Mascis from Dinosaur Jr for *Gas, Food, Lodging* (Allison Anders, 1992), Thurston Moore from Sonic Youth for *Heavy* (James Mangold, 1995) and *Things Behind the Sun* (Allison Anders, 2001), Billy Bragg for *Walking and Talking* (Nicole Holofcener, 1996), Stephin Merritt of the Magnetic Fields for *Eban and Charley* (James Bolton, 2000), Belle and Sebastian for *Storytelling* (Todd Solondz, 2001), Wilco's Jeff Tweedy for *Chelsea Walls* (Ethan Hawke, 2002) and Badly Drawn Boy for *About A Boy* (Chris Weitz and Paul Weitz, 2002).

In recent years there has been a move towards using sampling techniques in film music. Dance music DJ and producer, David Holmes, scored *Resurrection Man* (Marc Evans, 1998); adapting some of the film's underscore from his debut album *This Film's Crap, Lets Slash the Seats*. Holmes then went on to score two films for director Steven Soderbergh, *Out of Sight* (1998) and *Ocean's Eleven* (2001). The score to *Out of Sight* used sampling to include film dialogue and latin pop grooves; whilst *Ocean's Eleven* is a different type of compilation score, including original instrumentals, some of his own finest tracks and archive classics. Holmes has also composed a more traditional score for *Analyze That* (Harold Ramis, 2002).[9]

Other interesting developments have included the British band Asian Dub Foundation performing a new, live soundtrack for French film *La Haine* (Mathieu Kassovitz, 1995), American independent band Yo La Tengo providing a live soundtrack to the surreal short films of French director Jean Painlevé and US techno DJ Jeff Mills providing a score for a re-edit of Fritz Lang's *Metropolis* (1927).

Let us now explore some of the reasons for rock stars becoming involved in film music from two perspectives. Firstly, from the industry perspective of film directors and production companies; and secondly, from the perspectives of the musicians themselves. With regard to the industry, directors and film production companies may choose a rock star to compose a score rather than a more established film composer because they want a more experimental approach and/or they may want an established name from the pop world from which they can benefit in terms of marketing. There are also financial implications; it may be cheaper to have a score composed by a rock star, particularly if they will also perform most of the music themselves. Some directors love the work of a particular artist, for example director Cameron Crowe is a fan of musician Paul Westerberg, and, as we saw in the last chapter, director Paul Thomas Anderson is a friend and a fan of singer-songwriter Aimee Mann.

The reasons from the perspective of the popular musician are more complex. Most popular musicians who have made the move into film scoring have declared their passion for films and film music but there are other reasons to consider including the desire for artistic credibility, and the search for a new audience or a new creative direction. A number of popular musicians who have composed for film have said they are doing it because they have always wanted to, or because they love films and film music. French electronic duo Air composed the soundtrack to *The Virgin Suicides* (1999); director Sofia Coppola sent the duo the script and they were open to the idea saying, 'We've always wanted to do a soundtrack' (Roberts 2000: 84). British independent band Tindersticks worked with French director Claire Denis on soundtracks to two of her films, *Nénette et Boni* (1996) and *Trouble Every Day* (2001). Upon approaching the band Denis had been thinking of using previously recorded songs rather than an original score; however, Stuart Staples, the band's lead singer told her, 'It doesn't interest me that you use one of my songs, I'd like to compose an original score' (Anon. 2003).

Toop suggests that, 'For musicians, a composer credit on a movie conferred validation. This was as near as most rock stars would ever come to being a "proper" composer' (1995: 77). This idea will be discussed in further detail with regard to Damon Albarn later in this chapter. K. J. Donnelly has argued that a move to film scoring, 'was the logical conclusion of the trajectory of legitimisation for pop musicians, another way they could promote themselves as artists, and an increasingly attractive and viable option for musicians who were ageing' (2001b: 53). As mentioned previously, it is certainly true that composing for film can be used to revive a lagging pop career but there are also examples of newer, younger artists having made the move as well as those who still have a successful career. Whilst there is a relatively long list of pop musicians who have composed scores for the occasional film[10] there are fewer who have really developed a career out of this (for example, Clapton, Knopfler and Sakamoto); in addition most of these have continued their career in the rock/pop world. It would seem that the desire for a new direction is a concern for many of these musicians, and connected with this the desire for a new audience. Whilst their rock/pop careers have continued they are perhaps not as lucrative as they once were.

A number of popular-musicians-turned-film-composers have commented on how film scoring enables them to be more experimental. Stewart Copeland, ex-member of the Police has written over fifty film scores, his first for *Rumble Fish* (Francis Ford Coppola, 1983). He has said one of the attractions of composing for films is,

> The fact that I get to play with all these musical toys: I get to work with symphony orchestras, or with tiny little jazz ensembles. When you play pop music it's very exciting, but it has a very limited scope. (Copeland in Ross 2002: 38)

Mark Mothersbaugh, the ex-Devo leader, has his own company, Mutato, for which he has composed music for kid's TV shows and TV commercials as well as films including *Happy Gilmore* (Dennis Dugan, 1996), and Wes

Anderson's *Rushmore* (1998) and *The Royal Tenenbaums* (2001). He has described the transition to scoring 'a natural progression', saying that Devo were always inspired by films and were making films before there was MTV. Ex-Velvet Underground member and solo artist John Cale has composed a number of film scores, many of them for European films. Cale's first film score was for the Andy Warhol film *Heat* (1972); since then, in addition to his European soundtrack work, he has also composed music for a number of films directed by Jonathan Demme including *Something Wild* (1986),[11] two Mary Harron films, *I Shot Andy Warhol* (1996) and *American Psycho* (2000), and also composed a new score for Tod Browning's silent film *The Unknown* (1927). Cale sees more freedom in his European soundtrack work:

> They will try things over there that they wouldn't in other places. I can sit down and discuss several ideas and have immediate feedback, with Hollywood, they hire you if you are a 'package' ... A solo piano score is not something that interests somebody in Hollywood. They're interested in high volume. (Cale in Gassen 1995)

A number of directors who have collaborated with popular musicians on film scores have commented on the collaborative process. Smith notes how during the post-production phase of *Shaft*, director Gordon Parks received tapes of Hayes' music as he composed it, and made changes in his editing to accommodate the score (1998: 147–8). Denis completed the screenplay to *Nénette et Boni* while listening to Tindersticks and filmed certain scenes live to the music to help capture the right ambience. Denis has commented on how Tindersticks frontman Stuart Staples influenced the editing process of the film, 'Stuart and his music gave us more courage to be more elliptic, abstract ... The music uninhibited me so I could fabricate the film' (Anon. 2003). Jim Jarmusch has discussed how RZA's music was an inspiration on *Ghost Dog: The Way of the Samurai* (1999), and how RZA got them 'to work in a hip-hop style with the music' (Andrew 1999). And composer Mark Mothersbaugh has described the process of working with director Wes Anderson on *Rushmore*; Anderson was playing his songs on set while he was shooting and would also send Mothersbaugh music he was listening to.

For directors, working on a film can be an opportunity to work with others who share the same sensibilities and vision, and this applies equally to the composer as it does to the rest of the creative team.

Case study: Damon Albarn

Damon Albarn is the frontman of British band Blur. He is classically trained and writes much of Blur's material as well as singing lead vocals and playing keyboards and guitar. Blur was formed in London in 1989 and with each album they release have continually reinvented themselves. Initially an indie-dance band, during the Brit-pop era the band came into their own. The new, quintessentially British Blur released the *Parklife* album and 'Girls and Boys' single in 1994; the album went triple platinum and Blur became hugely successful. 1995 saw the battle between Oasis and Blur, hailed in the press as the 'Battle of the Bands'; Blur's single 'Country House' beat Oasis to reach number one in the singles charts. 1997 saw another change of direction; influenced by American bands such as Pavement and Sonic Youth, Blur released their self-titled album and the singles 'Beetlebum' and 'Song 2', all of which were hugely successful. 1999 saw yet another change of direction with the album *13*, produced by William Orbit. Whilst *Think Tank*, released in 2003, is an eclectic collection, including punk and dance as well as demonstrating Albarn's interest in world music and Blur's penchant for the ballad.

As well as his work with Blur, Albarn has been involved in a number of side projects. He collaborated with comic artist Jamie Hewlett and several leading hip-hop producers to create the manufactured rap and dub cartoon band Gorillaz, comprised of four animated characters. In addition Albarn became involved in world music, traveling to Mali to record with traditional musicians; the result was the album *Mali Music*, released in 2002. Albarn also began to get involved in film soundtrack work, writing the track 'Closet Romantic' for the end credits on *Trainspotting* (1996).[12] Since then Albarn has completed scores for three very different types of film. Albarn had his first major acting role in Antonia Bird's British crime thriller *Face* (1997) and had been keen on scoring that film as well; Bird was worried this may be seen as some kind of publicity stunt and declined but promised him the job on her next film. This was *Ravenous* (1999), a film about cannibalism; Albarn agreed to work on the music on the condition that established film composer Michael Nyman help him. 'He wanted me as a collaborator and hand-holder', says Nyman (in Sweet 1999). Albarn's next score was for the Irish gangster film *Ordinary Decent Criminal* (2000) directed by Thaddeus O'Sullivan and starring Kevin Spacey. Albarn then went on to collaborate with ex-Sugarcube Einar Benediktsson on the film *Reykjavik 101* (Baltasar

Kormákur, 2000), a drama set in the Icelandic club scene. Each of the three scores Albarn has worked on shows a different direction; I will now discuss each of these in turn.

The music for *Ravenous* reflects the sinister horror and irreverent humour in the film; according to Nyman it was Albarn who 'responded to the film's more gruesome moments' (Sweet 1999). The score is also reminiscent of Morricone's scores for the 1960s spaghetti westerns emphasising the sense of emptiness of the wild west where all of the characters are outcasts and use is made of many Old West traditional instruments with a modern twist to create an unmistakably distinctive sound. There is a combination of classic banjo 'chase music' complete with yodeling, Moog synthesisers, bluegrass rhythms and Native American laments; the dulcimer, a Russian instrument used by Morricone, is also used. In terms of influences Albarn had been listening to early American folk music from the Smithsonian collection; he also wanted to use authentic Native singers and was able to record the vocals of one of these singers, Quilt Man, whose sounds were inspirational, for Albarn and also for the sound designers on the film. The highlight of the score is at the end of the film; Albarn described working on this, saying he started writing and could not stop (DVD commentary). The eerie feeling Albarn was keen to get is achieved with a combination of low keyboards, chanting male voices and drums, appropriate for the climax of the film.

Ordinary Decent Criminal tells the story of Dublin's most notorious criminal Michael Lynch, played by Kevin Spacey. This is Albarn's solo film score debut and director O'Sullivan was keen for Albarn to do the music, as he wanted a pop score rather than a traditional classical score. O'Sullivan also commented on how it is usually the case that this type of film (urban gangster drama) uses pre-recorded music but he wanted a composer who could compose a score to cover the range of needs of the film. Albarn became involved in the film fairly late in the process and wanted to give the film a 'kind of folklorish quality' as Kevin Spacey had turned his character into a Robin Hood figure (O'Connor 2003).

Albarn composed two score passages, 'Chase After Gallery' and 'Bank Job', which both have a noir-ish sound. In addition he composed three solo tracks, each of which has a different feel but all of which experiment with sound. The seven-minute long, 'One Day at a Time' (a Kris Kristofferson song) is a collaboration with Massive Attack's Robert '3D' Del Naja, which uses trip-hop beats under Albarn's vocals. The second solo track, 'Kevin on a Motorbike', is slow with blues-like distortion. It is the third solo track which is the highlight, a gospel-inflected country ballad 'Dying Isn't Easy', which was written for the film's epilogue and uses strings, a gospel choir and acoustic guitar.

Albarn then went on to collaborate with Einar Benediktsson on *Reykjavik 101*. The film was directed, written and co-produced by Baltasar Kormákur who co-owns a bar in Reykjavik with Albarn. Albarn describes some of the music for the film as being partly improvised:

> Composers like Morricone and Barry were masters of taking some-thing contemporary at that time and transforming it into a film score, whereas most film music today consists of ready-made songs put on a soundtrack. We tried the same thing, and even had three themes following each of the main characters, which goes back to Morricone again ... I like to work with traditions and take them further in my own interest. (Albarn in Neiiendam 2000: 21)

Perhaps the most interesting theme used is that for the main character Lola, and there are no less than six versions of the Kinks song 'Lola' used – including a wonderful flamenco version. Much of the music has a clubby feel with some techno and some jungle music, and there are also hints of the urban style of Gorillaz.[13]

FIGURE 6 *Reykjavik 101* (Baltasar Kormákur, 2000)

We shall now explore the possible reasons for Albarn's involvement in film music using the reasons outlined earlier. Firstly, as with many popular musicians Albarn has a love of film and of film music, citing his favourite composer as Ennio Morricone. Writing for film is something he has been aiming towards for some time, having turned down a few big Hollywood-type projects in favour of projects he has a particular interest in (O'Connor 2003). But is this love of film enough to justify actually moving into that area himself? If the notion of moving into film music to gain artistic credibility is considered then it needs to be remembered that Albarn has progressed beyond the various incarnations of pop band Blur into world music and the rap and dub of Gorillaz. Surely these involvements would confer some kind of artistic credibility if that were the aim. Or is there a higher level of artistic credibility proffered to those who compose music for film? Albarn has received some criticism from the music press about his film scoring:

> If it's artistic credibility he seeks, then surely there are more scenic avenues than this ... If Damon has been lured to the cinema because his inspiration for the band has run dry, perhaps it's time he made a solo album instead. (Long 2000)[14]

Nevertheless it seems certain that the collaboration with Nyman on his first film score may have brought Albarn some artistic credibility in the film-scoring world and it is interesting that Nyman agreed to work with Albarn, in fact conferring a different kind of credibility on Nyman![15]

With regard to seeking to move into a new direction, as Toop has suggested, the entry to film scoring is a result of the adventurousness of pop musicians themselves – with Albarn it seems this certainly plays a large part: 'The grand realisation was that I was never going to be happy in this business unless I became far more committed to the actual music' (Albarn in Flynn 2000: 14). As with many popular musicians Albarn has a very definite creative need to explore new ground and diversify: 'I think everyone should go on to something different ... When I was a kid I was subjected to West Indian music, Indian music, European music, everything' (Albarn in Grant 1999). However, once again, what is also of interest here is that Albarn's musical output has been eclectic from various incarnations of indie pop, grunge and dance to the rap of Gorillaz and through to world music. So why the need or desire to score for films also? It may be that for Albarn film music offers the opportunity to incorporate this eclecticism into one piece of work, as a score can include orchestral music, sampling and pop songs as well as other influences. Whilst each of Albarn's film scores shows different influences it is his eclectic approach that brings them, and Albarn's other side projects, together. There is also the clear influence of different cultures in both Albarn's side projects and his film score work. His range of collaborations suggests his willingness to experiment with music of different genres and from different regions; from the minimalism of Nyman, to Icelandic club culture, traditional Mali music, and the rap and dub of Gorillaz.[16] In terms of the search for a new audience, Albarn is still very much involved with Blur and still has a successful career as a pop musician, so does not need to find a new audience for commercial purposes but maybe the search for a new audience is part of aiming for a different kind of artistic credibility.

I would suggest that the main reason for Albarn's involvement in film music is related to Albarn's image and star persona. Toop has noted how

> a major shift of emphasis takes place when a pop musician enters the film soundtrack world. Pop music is public. In most cases, a persona is required in order to 'present' the music to its market, and to varying extents persona and music can become indivisible. Film scoring is an invisible activity. (1995: 73)

It is necessary to define what the elements of Albarn's star persona are in order to consider how his involvement in film music may have changed this, or indeed Albarn himself may have wished to change it. Albarn's image is that of cool, hip masculinity which appeals to both a male and female audience, his laddish machismo appealing to the male Brit-pop audience, and his boyish good looks appealing to the female audience. This was particularly the case at the height of Blur's celebrity in the mid-1990s with Albarn being seen as an object of appeal for many screaming girls; a recent interview also noted that, 'the man is still ludicrously pretty' (Beaumont 2003: 35).

The difficulty any popular musician has with this is that of having their status as a musician overlooked because of their looks and one of the appeals of film music may be its anonymity. As Albarn has said:

> You don't have to use your face. I want to become anonymous. Not a complete recluse, but not have to ever sell myself on anything

other than my music, which in the pop business everyone has to do. (Albarn in Grant 1999)

Clearly connected to this is the celebrity lifestyle Albarn was living during the mid-to-late 1990s. An interview in *Dazed & Confused* magazine suggested the following:

These soundtrack diversions are becoming a pivotal escape clause from what could so easily have become the mythological life of Damon Albarn, year 2000. (Flynn 2000: 14)

Albarn was also criticised by the press for the personal nature of some of the tracks on the album *13* and has talked about the need to escape during this period of 'celebrity and tabloid craziness' (*The South Bank Show*); it may be that film music offers him an element of escape, as well as a way of expressing what is in the film rather than expressing himself.

Toop notes that the hierarchical nature of film marketing relegates the composer to a tiny credit at the bottom of the poster but with musicians of the stature of Albarn, whilst they may only have a tiny credit at the bottom of the poster, their score can be used as a major marketing tool for the film. The front of the DVD cover for *101 Reykjavik* prominently states 'Original Soundtrack by Damon Albarn & Einar Orn Benediktsson'; whilst on the back cover of the *Ordinary Decent Criminal* DVD 'Music by Damon Albarn of Blur' is stated beneath the film synopsis. There is obviously a benefit for the film company from using an artist such as Albarn to compose a score as audience identification with particular stars is an important marketing tool; and there are always a number of fans who will buy the soundtrack album and see the film purely because of the involvement of a particular musician.

Whilst authors have drawn attention to the use of pop music in film, only David Toop has directly addressed popular musicians composing for film. Other authors who have written about film music have briefly and critically mentioned the movement of pop musicians into film scoring. Perhaps none more so than Irwin Bazelon who commented on the score for *Shaft*:

Yes, the music worked – main title and all – but what doesn't in this kind of superman-exploitation film? In this light, anyone with the slightest visual-dramatic instinct can compose music for a film in one haphazard way or another. (1975: 32)

Popular musician Ry Cooder, who has composed for film, does not have much use for rock music in films, saying it is a narrow path which has more to do with performance:

> But I don't know about rock 'n' roll as score because it's so predict-able – like, how many things *are* there? When they start putting these pop songs into films, to me it just stops the film. It crashes, everything goes crash unless the film is about pop song. (Cooder in Romney and Wootton 1995: 121)

It is also the case that traditional film scores can be equally predictable. Bob Last, founder of British independent label Fast Product who has worked as music co-ordinator on a number of films, has suggested that one of the reasons why pop musicians moving to film scoring does not work is that,

> making the transition to score is a very loaded moment in terms of their own perceptions. They always see it as something where they should be seen to be *composing* in a way they would never burden themselves with if they were doing a song. (Romney & Wootton 1995: 127)

Meanwhile others have argued that using popular musicians to compose is a way of doing something new and different. Music supervisor and film director Alex Steyermark comments:

> Part of the fun for me is finding musicians who have never com-posed for film before and then giving them a chance to do it, like Dave Grohl of the Foo Fighters, who scored *Touch* [Paul Schrader, 1997], or Jeff Tweedy from Wilco, who scored *Chelsea Walls*. (Martin 2002b: 36)

In an article on popular musician Sting's career as a film star, Phil Powrie suggests that,

> the film personae of rock stars will therefore always already be fractured, whichever type of audience is being targeted. They are always 'out of place', disjointed, disarticulated. (2003: 87)

I would suggest that this is also the case with popular musicians who move into composing for film; whilst the urge to diversify musically may be satisfied, they will always be 'out of place'. These musicians have become known to the public through their persona as pop musicians and no matter how many film scores they compose they will always be seen as songwriters rather than composers. This may also explain why so many hold on to their career as pop musician as well as being involved in film scoring.

Consideration must also be given to the possibility that scores composed by pop musicians are being used as a marketing tool in the same way that songs have been used in compilation scores. Toop suggests that the use of pop song as soundtrack was seen by Hollywood as a device to maximise the cinema audience and create a youth cinema to match the ascendancy of rock in the latter half of the 1960s (1995: 75). Although it is important to note that this had also happened in the 1950s with rock 'n' roll. Ben Thompson considers examples of pop stars moving into acting roles in film;

> There is no mystery about the mutual attraction between film-makers and pop stars. Big pop names will – in theory at least – supply both charisma and crowds, and films offer them the chance to appear multi-faceted at the same time as prolonging their working lives beyond the whim of teen allegiance. (1995: 33)

This emphasises the symbiotic relationship between the film industry and popular musicians and may also account for the keenness of Hollywood to involve these musicians in composing film scores and for the increase in this from the 1970s onwards.

5   SYNERGY AND THE COMMERCIAL FUNCTIONS OF FILM MUSIC

Whereas chapter two examined the textual functions of film music, this chapter will examine its commercial functions. It will outline how cross-promotional strategies have been used from the early days of silent cinema to the present, emphasising one of the main themes of the book, the way in which music has been used as a marketing tool. There will be an overview of cross-promotional practices in the silent to sound era and then in the classical Hollywood era. The commercial implications of the increased use of popular music in film in the 1960s and the rise of the pop soundtrack in the 1970s will also be discussed. This is followed by a more detailed discussion of the rise of the concept of synergy in the 1980s, considering the emergence of new forms that helped define the concept and the experimentation with film music outside of the mainstream sector.[1] Following this is a detailed discussion of the development of the soundtrack as a cultural product and diversification of the soundtrack genre in the 1990s, with consideration given to the increasing fragmentation of the market into niche audiences.

1895–1930: The silent to sound era

There are examples of cross-promotional practices between different aspects of the entertainment industries from the beginning of cinema. Russell Lack suggests that film music survived its earliest beginnings due to its effectiveness as a marketing tool (1997: 8) and that the emergence of cue sheets 'represented the advent of a new form of synergy between owners of copyright properties such as films and published music' (1997: 29).

Outside of the US, in 1908 *L'Assassinat du Duc de Guise* was largely promoted on the basis of its high profile original score by Camille Saint-Saëns. In the US early cross-promotional efforts concerned the sale of sheet music and several exhibitors included song slides and singers as special attractions in their programmes: 'The singers were frequently employed by music publishers for the express purpose of "plugging" a particular tune' (Smith 1998: 28). Both the publisher and the exhibitor benefited from this as the exhibitor would sell copies of sheet music in the theatre and retain a small percentage of the money and also have the services of a quality singer for little or no cost whilst publishers gained increased promotion for their music.

The Birth of a Nation (1915) is one early example of synergy as after first being played by orchestras on tour with the film, the score was made available to theatres in printed copies and the policy of publication of a score for distribution with the film was adopted for many subsequent important American films.[2] In 1916 Thomas Dixon Jr's *The Fall of a Nation* made cinema history when it achieved the most profitable film/music tie-in with its Victor Herbert score, which became available as a piano arrangement (Hanson and King Hanson 1986: 28). 1918 saw the first attempt at coordinated cross-promotion when a title song was commissioned for Mabel Normand's appearance in *Mickey*. The song advertised the film with pictures of Normand on the sheet music and record cover and the song went on to become an unlikely hit. This practice continued throughout the 1920s; Alexander Doty notes how songs such as 'Diane' from *Seventh Heaven* (Frank Borzage, 1927), 'Sonny Boy' from *The Singing Fool* (Lloyd Bacon, 1928) and 'Singin' in the Rain' from *Hollywood Revue of 1929* were, 'merchandised on records, on the radio and in the form of sheet music to capitalise upon a film's high market visibility' (1988: 70–1).

1930–1960: The classical Hollywood era

Between 1930 and 1943, Hollywood's control of the music publishing industry and its employment of the industry's top songwriters prompted the film song's greatest period of success. Whilst many of these songs were from musicals there were also songs from westerns, romances and melodramas. From 1940 music display racks installed in newsstands across America displayed sheet music for sale, which led to a resurgence in sales. After the war the market for recorded music grew and by the late

1950s the sheet music market had collapsed and Hollywood moved its interests in cross-promotion from music publishing to records and radio, which led to the use of a new range of promotional strategies.

There were some isolated examples of soundtrack albums to films being released in the 1940s; for example, *Spellbound* (1945), with a score by Miklós Rózsa and *The Third Man* (1949), with a score by Anton Karas. But it was not until the late 1950s that the soundtrack album really emerged as a vehicle for cross-promotion. Trailers for *The Third Man* superimposed the following words over the film's credit sequence close-up of a zither, 'Featuring the famous musical score by Anton Karas. He'll have you in a dither with his zither', an attempt to sell the film through Karas' already-popular zither theme (Doty 1988: 71, 78[n]). There was also an emphasis on themes and the 1950s saw a number of monothematic scores. Perhaps the most well known of these being *High Noon* (Fred Zinneman, 1952), with its theme song 'Do Not Forsake Me, Oh My Darlin'' written for the film by Dimitri Tiomkin and sung by Tex Ritter. The marketing campaign for *High Noon* was of huge importance to the business of film music marketing. Jeff Smith describes how the centrepiece of the campaign was the six single releases of the theme song; radio and sheet music were also exploited and the campaign featured many of the components used in later promotions (1998: 59). In 1955 the song 'Rock Around the Clock' was used in the film *The Blackboard Jungle*; Doty notes how this 'demonstrated to shrewd independent producers the great promotional value of popular music in exploiting the youth market' (1988: 73). This then led to the song's title being used as the name of a low-budget teenpic musical in 1956.

Doty outlines how it was the exploitation filmmakers of the late 1950s and 1960s who were always more adventurous in the development and use of publicity gimmicks than the major studios and large independent producers. They set the stage for more mainstream producers in the use of music and songs for pre-release film promotion. Much of this was connected to the drive to target the youth market in rock 'n' roll films and beach party films; however, they were also aware that popular music could also be used in other less-specifically youth-oriented films. When the major companies began to use popular music their choices were limited to 'safe' ventures and well-known artists such as Elvis Presley and later the Beatles (1988: 73). Doty argues that this conservatism dictates a play-it-safe approach to film production and film promotion and has also restricted the types of music included in and used to promote films (1988:

76). This conservative policy means the use of well-known songs and established artists to sell both soundtracks and films. Economically there is little risk in using established artists and songs; however, this leaves little place for creativity in terms of the type of music used, and how it is used both in the film and to promote the film. As is the case in both the film and music industries it is usually the smaller, independent companies who are prepared to take a risk and try something new.

1960s: increasing use of pop music in film

In the early 1960s Henry Mancini's work, 'initiated some of the most significant changes in the industry, among them the recording of film music specifically for soundtrack albums' (Smith 1998: 70). Mancini was openly critical of existing industry practices of soundtrack packaging, believing that many were only successful in establishing a main theme, with the rest of the album being a collection of bits and pieces:

> For this reason, Mancini usually re-recorded his film music for separate distribution on albums. In doing so, Mancini believed his soundtracks gained a number of advantages in the marketplace. For one thing, the rerecording of his scores gave them a better fit within the strictures of radio formats ... Moreover, as Mancini noted, he was also able to 'impose a real form on the music and thus give the album buyer a sound value'. (Smith 1998: 78–9)

Smith describes the aggressive marketing campaign, which made the song 'Moon River', from *Breakfast at Tiffany's* (Blake Edwards, 1961), a success. A few months before the film premiered it was announced that the publishing company had already licensed twelve different recordings of 'Moon River' and implemented a national promotion plan. Mancini, and the song's lyricist, Johnny Mercer, even offered a number of marketing suggestions to record dealers and radio programmers. By 1966 over 240 recordings of the song had been licensed (Smith 1998: 77–8). Both the song and the album were a success, with Mancini's soundtrack remaining on *Billboard*'s album charts for more than 96 weeks (Smith 1998: 70).

   At the same time record companies explored new ways of re-packaging old film music; soundtracks for *Ben Hur* (William Wyler, 1959), *Mutiny on the Bounty* (Lewis Milestone, 1962) and *How the West Was Won* (John

Ford, Henry Hathaway, George Marshall and Richard Thorpe, 1962) all featured deluxe packaging, eye-catching cover art and booklets of full-colour film stills to enhance appeal. This period also saw pop musicians increasingly becoming involved in composing music/songs for film, which obviously had increased sales potential. John Mundy notes how, whilst the importance of title or theme songs and the synergistic potential of the soundtrack album had long been recognised by Hollywood,

> the sheer global scale of the Beatles' success cemented the alliance between the music and screen industries, confirming the crucial importance of the visual economy of popular music. (1999: 174)

This success encouraged the film industry to include more popular music in films. As we have seen, *The Graduate* used songs by Simon and Garfunkel as nondiegetic music and *Easy Rider* used a selection of rock and pop songs as score, whilst *Butch Cassidy and the Sundance Kid* (George Roy Hill, 1969) contained the Bacharach and David song 'Raindrops Keep Fallin' On My Head'. Songs from these soundtracks gained radio play, which had a positive effect on soundtrack sales. By the end of the 1960s soundtracks were no longer simply promotional tools but were extremely valuable musical commodities. The success of *The Graduate* and *Easy Rider* was extremely important in terms of advancing the use of rock and pop songs as dramatic underscore (Smith 1998: 55).

1970s: the rise of the pop soundtrack

The late 1960s and early 1970s saw a change in how music was being used both in film and to promote film. Following on from *Easy Rider*, a number of films used prerecorded pop songs as score; these included *The Last Picture Show* (Peter Bogdanovich, 1971), *Mean Streets* (1973) and perhaps most famously, *American Graffiti* (1973). Smith describes these compilation scores as being

> derived from a complex mix of music, marketing and cinema, the compilation score attains its importance as a commercially self-aware alternative to the neo-Romantic orchestral scores of Hollywood's 'Golden Age'. (1998: 155)

At the same time the blaxploitation genre of film emerged, and Lack describes this as being 'the only genre that has become defined by its musical soundtracks' (1997: 218). In 1971 Isaac Hayes' score for *Shaft* gained radio play and became a hit; this generated more publicity for the film and Hayes' score went on to win an Academy Award:

> The gradual realisation of new possibilities in music marketing began when film distributors and exhibitors saw that a song like Isaac Hayes' 'Theme From *Shaft*' … had a recognition value extending beyond the originally targeted audience. (Doty 1988: 74)

Both film production companies and record companies began to realise the promotional value of popular music and not just in Hollywood. In the UK producer David Puttnam made a deal with the record label Ronco for a film starring pop star David Essex, *That'll Be the Day* (Claude Whatham, 1973), 'whereby if they put up finance for the film, it would feature a certain amount of rock classics on the soundtrack, which Ronco could then release on a double-album' (Donnelly 2001b: 55). By the mid-1970s, the soundtracks market was divided into two – 'scores' versus 'songs', with the song soundtracks selling the most.

Doty describes Jon Peters' *high concept** promotional campaign for *A Star is Born* (Frank Pierson, 1976) as setting a model which was then followed by *Saturday Night Fever* (John Badham, 1977) and other films. The campaign comprised of the film, a single – 'Evergreen', a soundtrack album and a novel which used the same photograph of the two stars Streisand and Kristofferson on its cover. The soundtrack album was released only two weeks before the film opened, instead of several months in advance, as originally planned. Peters' plan was for both the single and the soundtrack to become hits before the film's premiere; whilst the single took longer than anticipated to reach the Top 10 it received frequent radio play which Peters acknowledged had much to do with the success of the film in its first week of release. This strategy was modified for *Saturday Night Fever*; the soundtrack album was released about six weeks before the film opened to provide more time for the first single, The Bee Gees' 'How Deep is Your Love', to move up the charts. Other tracks were also released as singles over the first few months of the film's release. Both film and soundtrack were an enormous success (Doty 1988: 75–6).[3]

Smith quotes a 1979 *Billboard* article stating the ingredients for a hit soundtrack included the following:

> Commercially viable music. Timing. Film cooperation on advance planning and tie-ins. Music that's integral to the movie. A hit movie. A hit single. A big-name recording star. A big-name composer. (1998: 198)

He goes on to say that whilst not all ingredients were absolutely necessary the absence of one or two could spell the difference between a soundtrack's overall success or failure (1998: 198). This criteria was to go some way to establishing a model for synergy in the 1980s.

1980s: new formats defining synergy and experimentation outside of the mainstream

Whilst cross-promotional strategies have been present since the early days of silent cinema, the concept of 'synergy' was not defined until the 1980s. The strategy of synergy is that the common cross-promotion of films and records could benefit both industries in almost equal measure. The concentration of resources outlined in chapter one gave rise to the concept of synergy as a thoroughgoing principle of corporate organisation:

> Where the term had earlier referred to the simple proposition of using music to sell movies and vice versa, it now came to cover a whole system of cross-promotional practices designed to reinforce the conglomerate structure both vertically and horizontally. (Smith 1998: 191)

In their article 'Synergy in 1980s Film and Music' R. Serge Denisoff and George Plasketes discuss how the mass media industries increasingly explored the potential for cross-promotion in the 1980s. They describe how music supervisor Danny Goldberg coined the term 'synergy' which went on to become a marketing buzzword during the 1980s (1990: 257).[4] Denisoff and Plasketes discuss whether synergy is a formula for success or industry mythology, concluding that there are many failures that have been over-shadowed by, 'synergy successes in the corporate consciousness such as *Top Gun* [Tony Scott, 1996] and *Dirty Dancing* [Emile Ardolino,

1987]' (1990: 274). Denisoff develops this view in *Risky Business* (1991), co-written with William D. Romanowski; examining the box office and chart performance of numerous films and soundtrack albums of the 1980s they argue that the type of symbiotic relationship described by synergy rarely happened. Smith is critical of Denisoff and Romanowski but points out that, 'the phenomenon continues to be a dominant industrial practice' (1998: 228).⁵ Smith also discusses the symbiotic relationship between the film and music industries:

> Applying the logic of synergy, film promoters reasoned that if expo-sure to a theme song or soundtrack album were effective in making the film a hit, a successful film would, in turn, spur further record sales and mechanical royalties. Film and record promoters debated whether the music sold the movie or the other way around, but it was clear to all concerned that both benefited from the success of its counterpart. (1998: 58)

As noted in the introduction, a great deal has been written about synergy in the 1980s; much of this has been concerned with whether the music is there purely for promotional reasons, as composer Danny Elfman has commented:

> The most disturbing trend of the past ten years with rock 'n' roll and movies … is the stress on soundtrack albums and which songs go into a movie, without considering whether the song does anything for the movie. (Elfman in Occhiogrosso 1984: 31)

As quoted earlier, 'Music that's integral to the movie' was listed as one of the ingredients in marketing a hit soundtrack and there are many cases, such as *The Big Chill* (1983), where the music used in the film works with the film's narrative; however, there are also other cases, such as *Beverly Hills Cop* (Martin Brest, 1984), where it is purely there for economic rea-sons.

Throughout the 1980s many promotional campaigns followed the cross-promotional model established by *A Star is Born* and *Saturday Night Fever* and in the early 1980s the emergence of two new formats changed the world of soundtrack promotion. These new formats were music video and the compact disc; the introduction of the CD in 1982 saw the reissue of a number of old soundtracks on the new format. However, it was the music video, along with the emergence of MTV in 1981, that radically changed cross-promotional strategies. As Smith notes:

> MTV's target audience was essentially the same demographic sought by film producers during this period. And since a music video could include either actual or additional footage from a film, it gave potential filmgoers a better idea of the film's stars, narrative, genre and visual style than an accompanying single or album would. (1998: 200)

Music video became an important tool for film promotion with certain scenes from films being ideally suited for adaptation to the music video format. The emergence of MTV meant the influence of pop music as a marketing tool became more pronounced in the 1980s; a point acknowledged by Bones Howe, a Senior Vice President of Music at Columbia Pictures in 1989:

> Basically [the film companies] are looking for additional exposure for the movie; a pop soundtrack is just another way of promoting and marketing the film ... the video that's showing on MTV is like a three-minute commercial for the movie ... A hit single is a great way of setting up the movie. (Howe in Mundy 1999: 225)

There were also numerous examples of films with hit singles, one of the first being *An Officer and a Gentleman* (Taylor Hackford, 1982) with 'Up Where We Belong' by Joe Cocker and Jennifer Warnes. Mark Kermode notes that the much-played video was essentially an advertisement for the film and that producers and distributors have been loath to overlook such potential free publicity (1995: 17). *Flashdance* (Adrian Lyne, 1983) provided the initial model for film and music video cross-promotion with an emphasis on MTV as a promotional vehicle for the film.[6] A large number of films followed *Flashdance*'s winning formula including *Footloose* (Herbert Ross, 1984), *Beverly Hills Cop*, *Pretty in Pink*, *Top Gun* and *Dirty Dancing*. The entire credit sequence of *Ghostbusters* (Ivan Reitman, 1984) was filmed in a recognisable MTV format for Ray Parker Jr's song and then played on MTV as entertainment, but entertainment that would encourage viewers to see the film (Hanson & King Hanson 1986: 28).[7]

In 1989 the high-profile release of *Batman* was complemented by the release of two soundtrack LPs, an orchestral score by Danny Elfman and a collection of songs by the popular musician Prince, an example of the synergy of Warner Bros. music and film companies.

Experimentation outside of the mainstream

Outside of the mainstream there was an increasingly experimental use of music in film. Jane Giles discusses some of the distinctions and similarities between the underground and the mainstream, identifying the major difference between the two as being that the mainstream promotes popular culture whereas the underground is exclusive. Giles makes an interesting point that one of the most significant similarities between mainstream and underground is the maintenance of a star system incorporating actors, directors and musicians. She uses the term 'outsider stars' to describe artists such as John Lurie, Nick Cave and Tom Waits, all of whom have had acting and composing roles in a number of films made outside of the mainstream (1995: 45–7). Using artists such as these gives exclusivity and a certain element of cultural credibility to film; in addition this type of music is often cheaper to acquire than more mainstream music.

Not only is mainstream music usually expensive – it can cost up to $15,000 to clear just one song for worldwide use (Martin 2002a: 72) – but the clearing process is a time-consuming and problematic process. New Wave Films' Peter Broderick advises filmmakers to use original music: 'You want to control your movie and you don't want to be held hostage by someone else who can say no' (Broderick in Martin 2002a: 72). As is often the case with independent filmmaking, a lack of financial resources can lead to further creativity and originality. Established composer Mark Isham, who has collaborated on a number of films with director Alan Rudolph, amongst others, has said:

> Independent films tend to have a more open mind to the composer having a unique approach to the picture. The lower budgets require more creative choices of small groups of instruments, imaginative orchestration and a blending of electronic and acoustic instruments. (Rudolph in Gallo 1997)

And K. J. Donnelly notes:

Alternative pop songs are a good way of differentiating cultural product in a mass market, of courting a specific audience through the use of fairly particular music, and additionally adding a level of 'hipness' to a film. Cult music works well with, and sometimes can be a defining aspect of, cult films. (2001b: 154)

Lee Barron uses the example of the two soundtracks for *The Matrix* (Larry and Andy Wachowski, 1999), saying it was the soundtrack comprising of tracks by performers such as the Prodigy and Marilyn Manson which was much more popular. He goes on to suggest that the motivation for an album that includes these kind of tracks is twofold:

First, such performers lend a controversial 'edge' and cultural credibility to the film. Secondly, if, as has been argued (Jenkins 1992), fandom constitutes an alternative social (and subcultural) community characterised by informed cultural consumption, the opportunity to tap into this fan community is potentially very profitable. (2003: 211)

Many cult artists have a small but enthusiastic fan base and are likely to purchase a soundtrack album featuring a track by a particular artist regardless of the film. This cultural credibility is apparent in the work of directors Jim Jarmusch and Wim Wenders, in terms of both their films and the music used in them. Both directors work primarily outside of the mainstream and have stressed the importance of music to their work; as well as having close working relationships with 'outsider stars' John Lurie, Nick Cave and Tom Waits.

Jarmusch has used Lurie to compose scores for a number of his films; Lurie also has major acting roles in both *Stranger Than Paradise* (1983) and *Down By Law* (1986); as well as composing the scores for these two films and for *Mystery Train* (1989). Giles describes Lurie as the much sought-after star of the New York underground filmmakers scene of the early 1980s. She emphasises his appearance and persona, 'Blessed with wasted looks and a desirable, drop-dead cool attitude, he personified the moment' (Giles 1995: 47). Whilst appearance is undoubtedly of importance in appealing to a cult market, this is not to undermine the importance of the music also. Royal S. Brown has noted that, 'Some of the most effective jazz and jazz-oriented scores of late have come from the pen of John Lurie'

(1994: 238). As well as Lurie's score *Down By Law* also features two songs by another 'outsider star' Tom Waits; Waits also has a major acting role in the film and went on to compose the score (with Kathleen Brennan) for Jarmusch's third film, *Night on Earth* (1991).

Sometimes the cult status of musicians can also help with funding for independent films; independent American director Allison Anders has commented on how getting money for a soundtrack helped finish a film. *Border Radio* (1987) had a score by John Doe from X and Dave Alvin from the Blasters and songs by Green on Red and Los Lobos:

> We went to Enigma Records and they gave us money to finish, because they could get songs by John Doe and Dave Alvin that they could never possibly afford otherwise ... They gave us finish-ing funds to finish the film, plus took care of all the licensing and everything for us. (Romney & Wootton 1995: 134)

Many directors who choose to work independently do so in order to keep creative control of all aspects of the film including the music. Jarmusch has commented on the conservative nature of film music: 'The world is so full of interesting, amazing music, so why do all the scores sound exactly the same?' (Jarmusch in Klein 2000). He realises that this is the Hollywood way and that the use of conventions is what people expect but Jarmusch himself has a 'pretty close idea of the kind of music or who I would like to make the music' when making a film. This is demonstrated in his eclectic choices of musicians; as well as using Lurie and Waits, he has also worked with Neil Young and RZA, a member of the Wu-Tang Clan.

Working within the mainstream, decisions about the use of music are often outside the control of the director whereas directors working inde-pendently usually have creative control. Cameron Crowe has described how he was told at the last minute that if he did not have hit music on the soundtrack to his first film, *Say Anything* (produced by Twentieth Century Fox, 1989) then it would not be marketed (Romney & Wootton 1995: 133).[8] This leads to questions about who chooses the music for a film, in terms of both the songs being used and the composer being used. Anders has described how in discussions with Mercury Records on her film, *Mi Vida Loca* (1993), she told them, 'The bottom line is, the kids in the neighbour-hood in the movie are the music consultants' (Romney and Wootton 1995: 135). The important point being not so much that the director should be able to choose the music but that the director is happy with and feels confident about the choices of music. This is more likely to happen when directors collaborate regularly with the same composers, musicians or music supervisors and have a degree of control over the music being used.

By the end of the 1980s the trend for marketing films through music had become institutionalised in both the mainstream and the underground. This was to continue throughout the 1990s with the increasing fragmentation of the market and the development of niche audiences.

1990s: the diversification of the soundtrack genre and fragmentation of the market

Many of the synergistic practices established in the 1980s continued throughout the 1990s. Smith uses the example of *Sleepless in Seattle* (Nora Ephron, 1993) to illustrate both the potential cross-promotional advantages of corporate synergy and the extent to which a single intellectual property can enhance the interaction of a corporation's hardware and software divisions:

> Recalling the vertical integration of the studio era, *Sleepless in Seattle* was financed by Sony's Tri-Star Pictures, distributed by the Sony Picture Corporation, and, at least in some areas of the country, exhibited in a Sony theatre. After completing its theatrical run, the film was subsequently distributed by Tri-Star Home Video where it might be played on a Sony videocassette recorder or television. The film also spawned a successful soundtrack album for Sony's CBS Records subsidiary, Epic Soundtrax, which perchance was played on one of Sony's tape or compact disc players. (1998: 192)

Disney has been widely acknowledged as being very successful in its implementation of synergy; during the 1990s five of the Academy Awards for 'Best Original Song' went to songs used in Disney films.[9] *The Bodyguard* (Mick Jackson, 1992) is a prime example of synergy in the 1990s; Whitney Houston made her acting debut for Warner Bros. in the film as well as singing three songs on the soundtrack. The soundtrack was released on Arista and sold more than 27 million copies worldwide. Not only is a production company and record company involved in the synergy equation here but also a publishing company, as the film features Houston's recording of a Dolly Parton song, 'I Will Always Love You'. *The Bodyguard* is one of a number of bestselling soundtracks from the 1990s featuring pop stars in acting and singing roles, others include *The Preacher's Wife* (Penny Marshall, 1996) also featuring Whitney Houston, *Evita* (Alan Parker, 1996) featuring Madonna; and *Men in Black* (1997) featuring Will Smith.

Smith outlines a number of different marketing techniques that were being used in the 1990s. For some 'event' films soundtracks packaged several different kinds of artists together in an effort to reach as many different radio formats as possible. For example, *Twister* (Jan De Bont, 1996) grouped hard rock acts such as Van Halen with country and western singers such as Alison Krauss. *Batman & Robin* (Joel Schumacher, 1997) offered an even broader mix with REM, Jewel and R Kelly as well as up-and-coming acts such as Soul Coughing. Whilst in films made by contemporary African-American filmmakers Spike Lee, John Singleton and Mario van Peebles the soundtrack often highlighted the ethnic background of the director and the film's main characters. Some soundtracks exploited a particular gimmick; *Honeymoon in Vegas* (Andrew Bergman, 1992) featured contemporary covers of songs associated with Elvis Presley. In other cases soundtracks emphasised unusual collaborations, *Judgment Night* (Stephen Hopkins, 1993) paired popular rap and heavy metal groups such as Public Enemy and Anthrax and *Grace of my Heart* (Allison Anders, 1996), a fictionalised account of Carole King's life, used well-known 1960s songwriters together with their more contemporary counterparts (Smith 1998: 207–8).

The 1990s also saw three major developments; firstly, the emergence of the soundtrack as a cultural product in its own right; secondly, the diversification of the soundtrack genre; and thirdly, the increasing fragmentation of the market into niche audiences.

Emergence of the soundtrack as a cultural product

> In recent years, the soundtrack album has become a genre unto itself, regardless of the quality, popularity or genre of the film, and sometimes with little or no relation to the narrative of the film. (Freccero 1999: 91)

Smith describes the pop compilation as being the 'linchpin of Hollywood's cross-promotional apparatus' suggesting soundtracks are, a relatively safe bet since they either bring together several golden oldies in one package, or they provide a convenient sampler of a particular genre or style ... casual consumers are more likely to purchase an album that contains many well-known performers rather than buy an entire album by an individual artist. (1998: 209)

The soundtracks for two Wim Wenders films, *Until the End of the World* (1991) and *Faraway, So Close* (1993), are both compilations but operate in a different way to those usually produced by the mainstream. Both soundtracks fit into Smith's second category of a convenient sampler of a particular genre or style. Wenders has worked with a range of artists who write songs for his films; these include a mix of cult artists such as Jane Siberry and the House of Love; and more mainstream artists such as Bono and U2 with whom he has built up a close working relationship. Wenders has also worked with a number of 'outsider stars'. *Wings of Desire* (1987) featured two tracks by Nick Cave and the Bad Seeds, the band appearing in the film as themselves; Cave also contributes to *Until the End of the World* and *Faraway, So Close.*[10] *Until the End of the World* has a soundtrack with new material from Talking Heads, Neneh Cherry, Lou Reed, Patti Smith, and REM amongst others. The cover of the CD clearly states 'Featuring New Material By...' and goes on to list the artists included in a prominent position on the CD cover. I would suggest that a soundtrack album such as this is bought, not just by the 'casual consumers' identified above by Smith, but also by fans of these particular artists who are often unable to obtain the track elsewhere. This also goes some way to explaining why this particular soundtrack was more successful than the film itself.

The soundtrack to *Faraway, So Close* also operates in the same way; most of the music was written for the film by artists chosen by Wenders himself. All of the artists he approached knew the story of the film and were asked to comment in one way or another on the film story. Music plays an integral part in the film; a new song by Lou Reed, 'Why Can't I Be Good', acts as a leitmotif for the film and 'Cassiel's Song' by Nick Cave, played over the end credits, sums up the whole story. All of the music used in the film is on the CD, including tracks from Lou Reed, Nick Cave, Jane Siberry, Laurie Anderson and U2, as well as Laurent Petitgand's orchestral pieces. Unusually, outside of the mainstream, there was also a single release from the album featuring Reed's 'Why Can't I Be Good', Cave's 'Faraway, So Close' and 'Chaos' by German artist Herbert Groenemeyer.

Whilst soundtracks for independent films may well differ from those of films made in the mainstream there is still an emphasis on marketing and economics. In many of the independent films discussed the music works as an integral part of the film text but also, by using cult musicians and having less of an emphasis on the financial side, and less input from a production company, it also works as a cultural product in its own right. This then informs cultural consumption in the subcultural community of fans and subsequently has an impact on sales. These films and soundtracks are operating on a different level to those in the mainstream; they are removed from the world of MTV and music video, there are usually no single releases and they are marketed in a different way. Nevertheless it is important to note that they are still marketed and the use of these 'outsider stars' in both composing and acting roles should not be underestimated in their appeal to cult audiences.

Diversification of the soundtrack genre

The late 1980s and early 1990s saw the diversification of the soundtrack genre and following on from *Batman*, the strategy of releasing more than one soundtrack album has become more common. The film *Dick Tracy* (Warren Beatty, 1990) had three soundtrack LPs: the large orchestral background score by Elfman, one containing 1930s-style pieces composed by Andy Paley, and a third (but the first to be released!) – the Madonna album featuring three songs written by Broadway composer Stephen Sondheim and performed by Madonna in the film. This trend continued throughout the 1990s; examples include *Addams Family Values* (Barry Sonnenfeld, 1993), *The Crow* (Alex Proyas, 1994), *Forrest Gump* (Robert Zemeckis, 1994), *The Matrix* (1999), *The Virgin Suicides* (1999) and *American Beauty* (Sam Mendes, 1999). In each case this reveals a division of the films' music into orchestral score and song compilation.

Smith's categories of contemporary film scores as outlined in chapter one still exist although there are now additional categories and new hybrid forms emerging. Examples of orchestral scores that feature one or two popular songs include *Titanic* (James Cameron, 1997) which combines James Horner's score with Celine Dion's 'My Heart Will Go On'; *Pearl Harbor* (Michael Bay, 2001) which combines Hans Zimmer's score with Faith Hill's 'There You'll Be' and *The Lord of the Rings: Fellowship of the Ring* (Peter Jackson, 2001) which combines Howard Shore's incidental music with

Enya's 'May It Be'. Examples of a score which mixes orchestral underscore with several pop tunes include *The Full Monty* (Peter Cattaneo, 1997) which combines Anne Dudley's score with pop songs from Gary Glitter, Tom Jones and M People; *Spirit: Stallion of the Cimarron* (Kelly Asbury and Lorna Cook, 2002) which combines Hans Zimmer's score with the songs of Bryan Adams; and *The Good Thief* (Neil Jordan, 2002) which combines an original score from Elliot Goldenthal with songs from Bono and Leonard Cohen.

A new category also emerged in the 1990s, that of CD releases of 'Music Inspired By' films.[11] Kermode has described

> the rise of a bizarre phenomenon in which two, or even three, music albums from the same film are released simultaneously, one featuring the score, another the songs, and yet another languishing under the weirdly conceptual banner of 'songs inspired by the movie'. (1995: 19)

He goes on to use *Four Weddings and a Funeral* (Mike Newell, 1994) as an example, saying it

> spawned a soundtrack album in which the entire incidental score is reduced to a five-minute medley, while a wide-ranging collection of classic pop love songs packs out the rest of the album. Almost none of these songs appears in the movie but, cleverly intercut with snippets of dialogue from the film, they have served as an extraordinarily successful promotional item. (1995: 19)

La Haine (Mathieu Kassovitz, 1995) had two soundtrack releases initiated by the director; one a more conventional soundtrack and the other of 'music inspired by' from top French rap acts. Problems with clearing tracks by Bob Marley and Isaac Hayes meant the first release was held up until after the film had opened in France with an adverse effect on sales. The director commissioned the second soundtrack himself; he approached eleven rap acts and asked them to create their own musical impressions of the script. This sold far better than the film soundtrack and boosted the film's profile considerably; there were also no rights to clear or buy (Duncan 1995: 12).[12]

Barron describes this phenomenon as 'a novel and audacious development' and cites *The X Files* associated album, *Songs in the Key of X* as being a notable example. The CD from the show appears to feature the personal choices of the show's creator, Chris Carter, some of which have been included in the show but many have not (2003: 214).[13] The most interesting example in terms of 'Music Inspired By', however, is *The Blair Witch Project* (Eduardo Sanchez and Daniel Myrick, 1999), 'perhaps unique, in that it is the musical soundtrack to a film that has no musical soundtrack' (Barron 2003: 215). Another interesting point about this soundtrack being its 'Enhanced CD' format containing 'rare and exclusive' film footage that can be accessed by personal computer. Barron describes this as being,

> a triumph of synergy, ably aided and abetted by contemporary technology. Indeed, the Enhanced CD illustrates the nature of synergy within a single product, through its seamless marriage of sound and image. (2003: 220)

The genre has also diversified further with some albums containing both 'Music From and Inspired By' the film, for example, *Mission Impossible II* (John Woo, 2000), *Spider-Man* (Sam Raimi, 2002) and *Scooby-Doo* (Raja Goswell, 2002). Other synergistic examples are soundtracks featuring exclusive tracks from bands. The soundtrack to *Spider-Man* includes various new specially commissioned songs; whilst the soundtrack to *Orange County* (Jake Kasdan, 2002) features a track by the Foo Fighters, only available on this soundtrack; a sure way of getting fans of the band to buy copies of the soundtrack and maybe see the film. An original soundtrack by Clint Mansell was released for *Requiem for a Dream* (Darren Aronofsky, 2000) and was then followed by the release of a 'remixed' version. The success of the soundtrack to the Coen Brothers' film *O Brother, Where Art Thou?* (2000) led to a concert being held in Nashville with performers who had appeared on the soundtrack and the release of a second CD called *Down from the Mountain*, by the performers from the *O Brother...* soundtrack and a film of the same name based on the concert.[14]

Baz Luhrmann's film *Moulin Rouge* (2001) uses a wide range of songs to tell much of the story and instead of hiring a composer to write original songs for the film, Lurhmann decided to adapt famous songs from the past. The music includes many rock songs from the past two decades; the range is eclectic in terms of genre and time period, so there is something there for almost every generation and every taste; very clever from a marketing viewpoint. In the film the songs are orchestrated with main vocals from the film's two main stars, Nicole Kidman and Ewan McGregor. Luhrmann hired Craig Armstrong to coordinate the orchestral material; Armstrong also composed underscore for those scenes where a song was not used. There have been two main soundtrack releases, both produced by Luhrmann himself and also a promotional album. The first album, released at the same time as the film, features different versions of the songs from those in the film. A second album was then released to tie in with the DVD release, this contained the orchestrated versions of those songs as they appear in the film. Armstrong's cues do not appear on either of these two albums and are only included on the promotional album. This remains an interesting case in terms of synergy; whilst the orchestral reworkings of the pop songs do provide the majority of music in the film surely Armstrong's score is also important and could have been made available on one of the two CD releases.[15]

Fragmentation of the market into niche audiences

During this period a number of smaller budget independent productions and mainstream productions have organised soundtrack albums to target a particular niche market. This is especially true of films attempting to exploit a popular musical trend, for example, the Warner Bros.-produced *Singles* (1992) used the grunge music scene of Seattle and independent film *All Over Me* (Alex Sichel, 1997) used Riot Grrrl, featuring a soundtrack from artists including Sleater Kinney and Babes in Toyland. *Singles* was made in early 1991 but was not released until 1992, after the explosion of the Seattle grunge music scene; its release then obviously meant to tie in with the popularity of this scene. Crowe had been keen to use music that was not commercial in the film and swore there would be no soundtrack album: 'The final irony is that the soundtrack that I never intended to be an album became an album, and was huge (Crowe in Romney & Wootton 1995: 146).

Other films were marketed using 'Generation X appeal'; this included mainstream and independent films, as well as those films produced in that area inbetween the independent and mainstream sectors. Universal's *Reality Bites* (Ben Stiller, 1994) was one of those films aimed at the 'slacker' or 'Generation X' market,

> a prime example of a project where film and soundtrack CD form
> part of one and the same marketing initiative ... looks like a con-

scious attempt to call into being its own target demographic; a
generation of media-literate post-teens adept at reading and at
ironically participating in MTV culture and its corpus of pop-history
knowledge. (Romney & Wootton 1995: 6)

Other films aimed at the same market include Richard Linklater's *Dazed
and Confused* (1993) and Kevin Smith's *Clerks* (1994). For films such as
Dazed and Confused, produced ostensibly in the mainstream but aimed at
a non-mainstream market, a successful soundtrack can help ensure they
capture an audience who may well be encouraged to see the film through
the music.

There are also attempts to attract audiences using 'nostalgia culture'
with films using cover versions of well-known songs by new artists, as is
happening in the pop charts. *Backbeat* (Iain Softley, 1993) exploited interest in the Beatles and portrayed them before they were famous; this film
had a 'supergroup' of American alternative rock musicians playing the
Beatles songs.[16] Whilst *Velvet Goldmine* (Todd Haynes, 1998) used re-
recordings of period songs to conjure up the 1970s, for example, Placebo
covering T-Rex's 'Twentieth Century Boy'.[17] *Boys Don't Cry* (Kimberley
Pierce, 1999) has ex-Shudder to Think member turned composer, Nathan
Larson cover the Cure's title song; and *Donnie Darko* (Richard Kelly, 2001)
has Gary Jules and score composer Michael Andrews cover Tears for Fears'
'Mad World', the latter becoming an unlikely Christmas number one in
2003. This use of cover versions attracts two markets – the new audience
for the film and the existing fans of the original tracks.

In both the film and music industries the independent sector experi-
ments with new styles of music and filmmaking as well as new promotional
strategies, if proved successful these are then adopted by the mainstream;
this process is often referred to as a 'crossover'. It is perhaps ironic that
some of the most well-known examples of successful film soundtracks
from the 1990s, are from films made on relatively low budgets, which
have then successfully crossed over into the mainstream. This includes
films such as *Reservoir Dogs* (1991), *Pulp Fiction* (1994) and *Trainspotting*
(1996). The influence of Quentin Tarantino is not to be underestimated
here; Tarantino has taken an alternative approach to the use of music in
his films, choosing to use relatively unknown archive music rather than a
composer, or well-known pop songs. Tarantino has stressed the importance of creative control, saying, 'I'm a little nervous about the idea of

working with a composer because I don't like giving up that much control' (Tarantino in Romney & Wootton 1995: 127).

Tarantino's first film, *Reservoir Dogs*, was produced independently on a budget of $1.2m, before being picked up for distribution by Miramax. Tarantino had chosen the songs for the film but needed a record deal to pay for the rights to the songs. He has described being turned down by record executives who told him, 'There's not a soundtrack here' and how, even when MCA became involved they told him, 'We'll do it if you put in one of our artists, so we can have something to push.' The group concerned was called Bedlam; Tarantino had already chosen all of the songs and they even offered to do a remake of 'Stuck in the Middle With You'; however, the group disbanded and Tarantino ended up with the soundtrack he originally wanted released on MCA (Romney & Wootton 1995: 135). Both the film and the soundtrack were successful and Tarantino's second film, *Pulp Fiction*, was produced and distributed by Miramax, with a production budget of $8m. The high-profile soundtrack to *Pulp Fiction* was released prior to the film: '*Pulp Fiction* has score but again I didn't work with a composer. We used surf music a lot as score' (Tarantino in Romney & Wootton 1995: 127). The soundtrack CD to *Pulp Fiction* went triple platinum and brought surf music to a whole new audience; it was digitally remastered and converted into a special 'Collector's Edition' to coincide with the release of the film on DVD.

The advantages of using relatively unknown music is that it brings the music to a new audience who do not have their own associations with the songs and it also overcomes many of the licensing problems which can occur with using well-known material. Of course, there can also be a disadvantage here in that many film companies do not want to use songs that do not already have associations for an audience. But Tarantino is very aware of marketing opportunities: 'If you use a song in a movie and it's right, then, you know, you've got a marriage. Every time you hear that song you'll think of that movie' (Romney & Wootton 1995: 131). Perfect synergy! The success of the soundtrack albums for *Reservoir Dogs* and *Pulp Fiction* certainly had a role to play in the cult status of the films and ultimately played a role in the films becoming crossover successes. The soundtracks also influenced a number of compilation albums featuring tracks from the films and other cult classics.

The British film *Trainspotting* was produced by Channel 4 on a budget of £1.7m. The music plays an integral part in the film and also worked very well in terms of cross-promotion. The soundtrack is comprised of alternative music featuring newly-recorded tracks by Britpop bands such as Primal Scream, Blur and Pulp as well as dance tracks from Underworld and classic alternative tracks such as Iggy Pop's 'Lust for Life' and Lou Reed's 'Perfect Day', a very marketable mix. The marketing campaign for both the film and album was based around the orange numbers logo featuring the six main actors and a slogan 'Believe the Hype!' It has been proposed that the marketing campaign for the film 'suggested an approach rarely associated with a British movie. It was marketed almost like a band or an album' (Roddick 1996: 10–11). A second soundtrack album was also released; this included some remixed tracks and others inspired by the film. This release continued the successful 'brand identity' of *Trainspotting*, using the same logo but differentiating itself with the use of the colour green.

In the 1990s brand identities have become increasingly important; particularly in the mainstream and can be identified across a range of products. As Smith has suggested:

> Film's centrality to the synergy equation, however, has gradually been weakened by the emergence of new media and new cultural forms. With the progressive development of markets for home video, video games and home computer software, film is now simply one element in a much larger set of intellectual properties. (1998: 192)

Whilst this may well be the case within the mainstream I would argue that the relationship between music and film in the independent sector is just as important as it ever was, if not more so. The reason for this being that in the independent sector the film and the film soundtrack are often the only products available; lower-budget independent films do not tend to have the range of merchandising possibilities available in the mainstream. However, this is not to underestimate the huge impact new media and cultural forms have had on the mainstream film and music industries. If the last decade has seen the increasing importance of the soundtrack as a cultural product in its own right will the new multi-media technologies mean the death of the soundtrack as a cultural product? This question will be explored in the following conclusion.

CONCLUSION

In this conclusion I will firstly sum up the main debates surrounding film music considering industry organisation, technology, critical attitudes, textual conventions and commercial functions. This will incorporate the three main themes of this book; firstly, the prevalence of popular music in film since the beginning of cinema; secondly, the perceived superiority of the original score and the assumption that films need original music; and thirdly, the use of music as a marketing tool in film, also since the beginning of cinema. I will then discuss some of the challenges facing film music, as well as those facing academics and students interested in this field.

In terms of industry organisation a new industrial base is now in place in the mainstream Hollywood film industry, that of the global multimedia conglomerate. Most of the major film companies are now part of these conglomerates, which are involved in a range of activities across different media. The merger of AOL Time Warner is perhaps of most significance here, although it is not yet clear how the merged company will use its multimedia potential. Outside of Hollywood there is still a strong independent industry operating alongside these global multimedia conglomerates.

There is a clear distinction between those films produced by a major studio for a mass market and exhibited in multiplex cinemas, and those produced independently for a niche audience and exhibited in art-house or repertory cinemas. However, the distinction between the music used in the films produced by these two different institutions is less clear. Many of the films shown in art-house cinemas are seen as 'art films', but they often use a wide range of music, both popular and classical as demonstrated in the films of the New German Cinema discussed in chapter two. Many films produced for a mass audience use a conventional orchestral score and often popular music as well, so the relationship between films and their music are constantly being intermixed. What is clear is that the organisation of the industry and the institutional context in which a film is produced has always had, and will continue to have, a significant effect upon the type of music used in film and the way in which it is used.

The opportunities provided by digital technology have huge implications for both the film and music industries. The rise of the Internet and the popularity of music downloading services such as Napster have had a major impact on the music industry, although opinions are divided about whether this is an opportunity or a threat. The same technology enables films to be downloaded, yet it remains to be seen what the impact of this will be on the film industry. For film soundtrack CDs multimedia technology offers enhanced CDs which offer the possibility to connect to a film's official website. *The Matrix Reloaded* soundtrack CD released in 2003 offers two discs that contain film trailers for the movies, *The Animatrix* and the videogame, as well as songs inspired by the film and music from the film. The *Kill Bill* soundtrack CD, also released in 2003, is an enhanced CD with a teaser and two new trailers for the film.

Perhaps the most important technological development in recent years is that of the DVD. DVDs have been heavily promoted from the late 1990s; usually offering additional material to the VHS release, in the form of directors' cuts, commentaries, extra features, games and links to websites. Some offer the possibility for interactive engagement where viewers can re-edit sample scenes for example. There is also the occasional possibility of isolating the score; for example the US DVD release of *Amadeus* (Milos Forman, 1984) in 1997 offered an alternative music-only track. Lee Barron notes how the DVD version of *The Ninth Gate* (Roman Polanski, 1999) allows the users to isolate the incidental score suggesting that this 'may herald the start of a process in which, if the DVD continues to displace video, purchase of the official soundtrack might similarly become redundant (2003: 222).

Royal S. Brown predicted this to some degree in 1994, even before the rise of the DVD, noting how the laser-disc reissue of Roman Polanski's *Chinatown* (1974) offered the possibility of isolating Goldsmith's musical score from the soundtrack (1994: 265). He went on to discuss how CD-ROM technology allows considerable manipulation of textual material, which is already beginning to include movies, through one's personal computer. And if the music track can be separated from the rest of the soundtrack for home video, there is no reason why it will not eventually become possible to turn it off altogether and replace it by whatever music the viewer/listener would choose, including his or her own creation. (1994: 266)

Now this manipulation is readily available on DVD also. So what does the future hold for films and film soundtracks? Will this mean the death of the soundtrack as a product in its own right? Will there just be one product for the audience to purchase for home use? A DVD with separate music tracks for audiences to manipulate as they wish would enable audiences to interact with the product. There is also the possibility of downloading music via the Internet and for audiences to produce their own CD with their own choices of music. At the time of writing the choices offered by the film industry are still limited and predetermined to some degree. Whereas the choices made available via the Internet 'illegally' offer far more possibilities and has significant implications for the film industry. It may well be the case that if the industry does not formally offer the choices audiences want then audiences may take it upon themselves to provide themselves with the music they want, as has happened in the music industry. Whilst a music track on film rarely includes songs in full, the majority of songs are available to download on one of the many sites set up illegally for the downloading of music. A review of the *Spider-Man* soundtrack, which features 19 tracks, including some cues by score composer Elfman, stated:

As to whether these songs hang together as a decent compilation, the whole thing isn't too far off what you might get on a CD-R repre- senting one music fan's afternoon spent downloading MP3s from Audiogalaxy. (Robinson 2002)

It seems unlikely that the new media conglomerates would be happy to lose the film soundtrack and this may be one of the reasons why so few DVDs have offered the possibility to isolate the music score. Nevertheless audiences still have the option to download music via the Internet and create their own soundtrack to a film. As has been the case throughout history new technologies are exploited commercially but they are also often used directly by audiences in ways not intended.

Whilst recent writing on film music has placed more of an emphasis on compiled scores and the use of popular music there are still two areas of concern. Firstly, the fact that most writing about film music is from either a musicology or a film studies perspective and the two methodologies are often in conflict with each other; secondly, the assumption that orchestral music is 'better' than popular music. Recently authors have drawn attention to the divide in writing on film music and collaborations are now emerging between the two fields, it will be interesting to see what the outcome of a collaborative approach such as this will be. With regard to the perceived superiority of orchestral music, Corey K. Creekmur notes:

> Many recent studies of film music only gesture – often dismissively
> – toward the standard contemporary film soundtrack, which typi-
> cally maintains an instrumental score while emphasising a more
> sonically and commercially prominent selection of discrete pop
> songs, whether new or old (and often both), frequently including
> highlighted title and end-credit numbers. (2001: 382)

Even when scores that include popular music are mentioned, two general assumptions are made; firstly, that the popular music score is inferior to the orchestral score; this is linked to the second assumption, that classical music is original and popular music is not. One of the main intentions of this book has been to challenge these assumptions and point out that popular music can also be original, in many cases it is written specifically for a film; a score composed by a popular musician can also be more 'original' and creative than one composed by an established orchestral composer.

Contemporary film music is now far more varied than ever before. The conventions vary widely although many contemporary scores are comprised of both orchestral music (sometimes original and sometimes pre-existing classical pieces) and popular music (again sometimes original and sometimes pre-existing songs). The distinction between diegetic and nondiegetic music still exists although, as mentioned in chapter one, the boundaries are becoming increasingly blurred. This distinction also implies that diegetic music is popular music and that nondiegetic music is orchestral. James Buhler notes how this distinction was reinforced institutionally and still survives in the separation of credits for composers and songwriters. He suggests that the lack of theoretical interest in source or diegetic music is 'a lingering cultural elitism: orchestral music is where the art is' (2001: 43). This is despite the fact that popular music has now been used nondiegetically for over thirty years, yet this hierarchy of cultural values still exists. John Mundy makes an interesting comment about contemporary film soundtracks:

> It is important to recognise that this situation in which soundtracks for contemporary films are increasingly a mixture of existing songs and performances, together with numbers written expressly for a particular film, is not altogether too far removed from those two principal methods of film scoring, compilation and original composition which Marks identified as central to early 'silent' cinema. (1999: 226)

Another of the main intentions of this book has been to demonstrate that popular music has been an important part of film music since the beginning of cinema. This often seems to be neglected in writing on film music with the assumption that the use of popular songs in film is something that developed with *The Graduate* in 1967 and was then exploited, reaching a peak in the 1980s.

Writing on postmodernism has noted how the texts and practices of high culture have become mixed with the texts and practices of popular culture, 'to the point where the line between high art and commercial forms seems increasingly difficult to draw' (Jameson 1985: 112). Fredric Jameson discusses how postmodernism marks the end of individualism and cultural practices of high modernism and moves into the world of pastiche:

> In a world in which stylistic innovation is no longer possible, all that is left is to imitate dead styles, to speak through the masks and with the voices of the styles in the imaginary museum. (1985: 115)

Postmodern culture has been described as a culture of 'intertextuality' – rather than original cultural production there is cultural production born out of other cultural production. This is demonstrated in film music by scores partially born out of other film scores, composers and music supervisors choosing a range of music – some original, some pre-existing, some classical, some pop in order to give what Peer Raben described as 'additive originality' (Flinn 1994: 110).

This book has also attempted to demonstrate that the use of film music is not just textual and that music has always been used as a marketing tool in film. With the advent of synergy and the move to conglomeration, the marketing approach has become much more sophisticated and companies are constantly seeking alternative marketing strategies. Music plays an important role in attracting a particular audience to a film and a film soundtrack. The commercialism of the film music industry has also been associated negatively with the increase of popular music in film. As Creekmur notes:

> since most entertainment companies are linked by intricate corporate ties, what might appear as aesthetic choices (choosing and placing songs that best serve the meaning or mood of a film) are very often straightforward marketing decisions, designed to showcase musical acts on a media conglomerate's roster or to reinvigorate songs already in its catalogue. (2001: 385)

Whilst this is the case in the mainstream film industry, in the independent sector decisions about the use of music may also be made with the intention of showcasing music that has a particular cult audience.

There are a number of challenges facing film music and those academics and students interested in the field. Firstly, the role of music in the soundtrack, as lines become increasingly blurred between music and sound effects. More attention needs to be paid to the role of each of the three elements of the soundtrack; Rick Altman's work on *mise-en-bande* should be pursued so that the term becomes as familiar in film analysis as that of *mise-en-scène*. This would also encourage more people to feel confident in writing about music in film, particularly those who are not musicians or musicologists.

Most of the discussion here about writing on film music has centered around specific books on film music; yet many general film studies text books barely mention the music or the soundtrack – the emphasis is firmly on the visual. Surely this imbalance needs to be addressed – the soundtrack, and the music as part of the soundtrack, is an integral part of the filmic text; audiences need to be aware of how both visual and aural elements of a film operate in order to fully understand a film text. There is also a need for further discussion of the uses of diegetic music and its affective role on characters within films.

A major challenge is to revisit Claudia Gorbman's groundbreaking work; there are three main points that need to be reconsidered. Firstly, the idea that music is unheard; secondly, that action and dialogue stop for the duration of the performance of a song; and thirdly, consideration of the question 'Has it become "normal" to listen to a rock song with lyrics at the same time as we follow a story?' (1987: 163). In 1982 David Ehrenstein and Bill Reed suggested that after *American Graffiti*, 'the sound of rock in the movies would no longer mean that the action would have to come to a halt' (1982: 67). Whilst a number of directors have realised this and are increasingly using pop songs that work as an integral part of the dialogue and are often especially composed for the film rather than being chosen, it seems that this is still a problematic area in studies of film music.

Perhaps the most significant challenge to film music is that brought by digital technology and whether or not this will lead to the diminishment of the soundtrack as a cultural product or even to the death of the soundtrack. Russell Lack discusses how Roland Barthes proposes the notion of the death of the author, making the viewer the most important interpreter of the text, saying this 'paradoxically liberates the music, to be reclaimed by the unique perspectives of each listener-viewer' (1997: 230). New forms of technology are now enabling the listener-viewer to interact with the text thus giving them more control. This, along with an experimental use of music outside of the mainstream film industry, and the sense of playfulness engendered by postmodernism, has enabled a move away from the standardisation prevalent in the classical Hollywood era and given a renewed sense of creativity to film music.

Just as there are audiences for art films and for popular Hollywood films so there are audiences for the different variants of film music. Writing on film music must address the assumption that a mass-market film means a commercially successful popular music soundtrack; or that an art-house film means a soundtrack, which can be appreciated for its aesthetic value but will not be commercially successful. Surely it is now possible for both orchestral soundtracks and soundtracks comprised of popular music to be appreciated on an equal basis aesthetically. It is also the case that a number of orchestral soundtracks have been commercial successes. The orchestral soundtracks of composers such as Max Steiner, Bernard

Herrmann and John Williams, each with their own style of composition, are thought of as classics by critics and audiences alike. Likewise the 'pop' soundtracks of *American Graffiti*, *The Graduate* and *Easy Rider* are also thought of as classics by a new generation of critics and audiences for their innovative use of popular music.

It is important to recognise that music is one element of filmic creation and is best considered in relation to other areas of film analysis such as *mise-en-scène*, editing, and so on. In contemporary film it is becoming increasingly difficult to separate the textual and extra-textual elements of film music; decisions about the placing of music in film will always be coloured by the synergistic potential of the music – be it classical or popular. The soundtrack is truly a part of synergy.

NOTES

INTRODUCTION

1   Journals include *Film Score Monthly*, *Music From the Movies* and *Soundtrack!*. Web sites include www.filmsound.org/filmmusic, www.filmmusic.com, www.filmscore monthly.com and www.celluloidtunes.com.

2   Kassabian (2001) also discusses this problem, pp. 9–10.

3   Examples include *Blue Velvet* (David Lynch, 1986), *Pretty in Pink* (Howard Deutch, 1986), *Stand By Me* (Rob Reiner, 1986), *Pretty Woman* (Gary Marshall, 1990) and *Boys Don't Cry* (Kimberly Pierce, 1999).

4   The Dogme 95 'Vow of Chastity' states that music must not be used unless it occurs where the scene is shot.

CHAPTER ONE

1   These included performances from George Jessel, who was then playing in the Broadway production of *The Jazz Singer*, and Al Jolson, who performed three numbers.

2   See Altman 2001: 19 for more on this.

3   Meisel's score was not the only one, nor the first, for the film. See Prendergast 1992: 14 for more details.

4   In *Pop Music in British Cinema* K. J. Donnelly also uses the terms 'ambient diegetic', 'the performance mode' and 'the lip-synch mode' to discuss the appearance of music in film.

5   See Gorbman 1987 (chapter three) for a detailed discussion on the continuation of music into the sound film.

6   See Daubney 2000 for a thorough overview of Steiner's work.

7   Both Newman and Alex North used jazz for films set in New Orleans, *Panic in the Streets* (Elia Kazan, 1950) and *A Streetcar Named Desire* respectively.

8   Hughes directed, wrote and produced *The Breakfast Club* and scripted and executive produced *Pretty in Pink.*

9   See J. C. Buhler, C. Flinn & D. Neumeyer (eds) (2000) *Music and Cinema*; K. J. Donnelly (ed.) (2001) *Film Music: Critical Approaches*; A. Knight and P. Robertson Wojcik (eds) (2001) *Soundtrack Available*; K. Dickinson (ed.) (2003) *Movie Music: The Film Reader*; I. Inglis (ed.) (2003) *Popular Music and Film.*

10   It should also be noted that Bazelon was also critical of mickey-mousing in the work of Max Steiner, saying this often, 'vulgarised the scenes he was scoring' (1975: 24).

11   See Brown 1994: 67–91 for a number of close readings discussing the narrative power obtained by blurring distinctions between diegetic and nondiegetic music.

12   See Kalinak 1992: 184–202.

13   See Smith's case study of *American Graffiti* (1998: 172–85).

CHAPTER TWO

1   As much of the writing on the functions of music in film concentrates on the nondiegetic score in the classical Hollywood film, the focus here is on the diegetic and nondiegetic functions of music in contemporary film. For more on the functions of music in the classical Hollywood film see Gorbman's analysis of classical Hollywood practice using the scores of Max Steiner (1987: 70–98); Kalinak's analysis of *Captain Blood* (1939), *The Informer* (1935) and *The Magnificent Ambersons* (1942) (1992: 66–158); and Marks' discussion of *The Maltese Falcon* (1941) and *Casablanca* (1942) in Buhler *et al.* (2000).

2   In an interesting recent development Rick Altman has proposed an analytical model of the *mise-en-bande*, an acoustic equivalent to the *mise-en-scène*, which raises important points about the overall composition of the soundtrack. See Altman, Jones and Tatroe (2000).

3   See London 1936: 37, Gorbman 1987: 76, Smith 1996: 230 and Levinson 1996: 250.

4   Composer and theorist Roger Spottiswood's functions are outlined in Lack: 112. Also see Manvell & Huntley 1975, Karlin & Wright 1990 and Levinson 1996, the latter discussing art films as well as classic Hollywood.

5   Gorbman notes that counterexamples of music inappropriate to the mood are usually comedic or self-reflexive (1987: 78).

6   See Manvell and Huntley 1975 and Evans 1975.

7   Films scored by Elfman include *Beetlejuice* (Tim Burton, 1988), *Dick Tracy* (Warren Beatty, 1990), *Batman Returns* (Tim Burton, 1992), *Dead Presidents* (Albert and Allen Hughes, 1995), and *To Die For* (Gus Van Sant, 1995), *Spy Kids* (Robert Rodriguez, 2001), *Planet of the Apes* (Tim Burton, 2001) and *The Hulk* (Ang Lee, 2003).

8   K. J. Donnelly has written an interesting and useful article on Elfman's scores for *Batman*

and *Batman Returns*, 'The classical film score forever? *Batman*, *Batman Returns* and post-classical film music', in S. Neale (ed.) (1998) *Contemporary Hollywood Cinema*.

9   Gorbman notes how Giorgio Moroder's score in 1983 for Fritz Lang's *Metropolis* (1926) provides an interesting counterexample of the standard practice of segregating song lyrics from dialogue and significant action.

10 *Dark Habits* (1983) uses music by Miklós Rózsa and Bernard Herrmann, whilst *Labyrinth of Passion* (1990) uses the music of Nino Rota. Both *What Have I Done to Deserve This?* (1985) and *Law Of Desire* (1987) use 'La soledad de Gloria' ('Gloria's Solitude'), by Bonezzi.

11 The film is a true story of Sybille Schmitz, a film star in Hitler's Germany, who died of her addiction to morphine.

12 *Who's That Knocking at My Door?* (1968) and *Mean Streets* (1973) both had scores of popular songs. *Taxi Driver* (1976) was scored by Herrmann, *The King of Comedy* (1983) and *The Color of Money* (1986) by Robbie Robertson, *After Hours* (1985) by Howard Shore, *The Last Temptation of Christ* (1988) by Peter Gabriel, *The Age of Innocence* (1993) and *Bringing out the Dead* (1999) by Elmer Bernstein and *Kundun* (1997) by Philip Glass. Scorsese rejected the score composed by Bernstein for *Gangs of New York* (2002), instead choosing to use an eclectic collection of pop, folk and neo-classical music supervised by Robbie Robertson.

13 The CD soundtrack released featured less than half of these tracks.

14 In an interview with Gavin Smith in *Film Comment*, Smith says to Scorsese: 'Pop music is usually used in films, at least on one level to cue the audience to what era it is.' To which Scorsese responds: 'Oh, no, no, forget that, no!' (1990: 29).

15 See Noel Carroll 'The Future of Allusion', *October*, 20, Spring 1982, 51–81.

CHAPTER THREE

1   Jeff Smith notes how in the late 1970s film scripts were developed based on songs such as the Eagles' 'Desperado' and Elton John's 'Goodbye Yellow Brick Road' but did not reach the screen (1998: 199).

2   Interestingly, jazz musician Dave Grusin provided half of the film's music but is often not mentioned in the many articles written about music in the film; the credits state 'additional music by Dave Grusin'.

3   Directors often become attached to music they use as a 'temp score'. Perhaps the most famous example of this is that of Stanley Kubrick's *2001: A Space Odyssey* (1968), where the director replaced a score by Alex North with the selections of classical music he had become attached to as a 'temp score'.

4   *The Long Goodbye* (1973) had a title song composed by John Williams which is almost the only song in the film and is played in a wide variety of styles. For *Nashville* (1975)

Altman had the cast write and perform their own songs. Altman used Harry Nilsson and Van Dyke Parks to score *Popeye* (1980).

5   Not only that but Cohen insisted Columbia Records let Altman use his music for free as well as giving him a percentage of all subsequent sales of his record after the movie was released. ‹html://www.cduniverse.com/productinfo.asp?style=movie&PID=1262874&frm=sh_google.html› (10 May 2002).

6   'Dyslexic Heart' was released as a single in the US with a video directed by Crowe.

7   Interestingly only songs from Seattle-based artists are featured on the soundtrack CD; other music used in the film from non-Seattle-based artists such as the Pixies, REM and Public Enemy is not featured, nor is any of Westerberg's instrumental score.

8   Both films had scores composed by Michael Penn (husband of Aimee Mann); in addition *Boogie Nights* also includes a number of period songs from the 1970s. See Smith's article 'Popular Songs and Comic Allusion in Contemporary Cinema', in A. Knight and P. Robertson Wojcik (eds) *Soundtrack Available* (2001) for an interesting study of the use of songs as musical puns in *Boogie Nights*.

9   Orchestral score composer Jon Brion contributes to this track.

10 Brion also contributes to this track.

11 Gabrielle's 'Dreams' is not featured on the soundtrack CD.

12 Director Mike Figgis tells an interesting story about this on *Leaving Las Vegas* in 'Silence: The Absence of Sound', in L. Sider, D. Freeman & J. Sider (eds) (2003) *Soundscape: The School of Sound Lectures 1998–2001*, London: Wallflower Press, 4–5.

13 'Wise Up' was used in *Jerry Maguire*, *Whatever* was named after a Mann song and Mann sings 'I Should've Known' in the film. Mann also sings a Beatles song in *I Am Sam*.

14 Bramson was also music supervisor on *Singles*.

15 In addition Mann's soundtrack was nominated for 'Best Compilation Soundtrack Album' at the Grammy's; Brion's score also received a Grammy nomination for Best Score Soundtrack album.

16 One of the film's production designers, Mark Bridges, described how the film is very much about a time and a place – 1999 San Fernando Valley – saying they approached the film as a period piece and Mann's songs contribute to this. See www.magnoliamovie.com/infoMIDprd.html (17 January 2003).

CHAPTER FOUR

1   Numerous pop and rock stars have performed in films including Elvis Presley, The Beatles, Sting, David Bowie, Damon Albarn and many others. Rockumentaries include *Don't Look Back* (D. A. Pennebaker, 1967), *Gimme Shelter* (Albert Maysles/David Maysles/Charlotte Zwerin, 1970) and *Ziggy Stardust and the Spiders From Mars* (D. A.

Pennebaker, 1973). Mark Sinker discusses bands naming themselves and their releases after films in 'Music as Film' (1995: 117[n]).

2   Adamson went on to work on *The Last of England* (Derek Jarman, 1987), *Gas, Food, Lodging* (Allison Anders, 1992) and *Lost Highway* (1997).

3   The article by David Toop in *Celluloid Jukebox* is the only article to date to discuss this.

4   See K. J. Donnelly (2001) *Pop Music in British Cinema*, for more on this.

5   McCartney returned to film with the song and main theme for the Bond film *Live and Let Die* (Guy Hamilton) in 1973, he also composed a song especially for *Vanilla Sky* (Cameron Crowe, 2001) and Beatles songs have been used in numerous films.

6   Tangerine Dream also scored *Thief* (Michael Mann, 1981) and *Legend* (Ridley Scott, 1985). Director Ridley Scott was forced by a Universal Executive to scrap composer Jerry Goldsmith's score for *Legend* in favour of a soundtrack by Tangerine Dream in order to attract a youth audience (Romney & Wootton 1995: 19).

7   Cooder has composed scores for a number of Walter Hill films including *The Long Riders* (1980), *Southern Comfort* (1981), *Streets of Fire* (1984) and *Johnny Handsome* (1989) as well as working with other directors.

8   This was a collaboration with Graeme Revell.

9   Chapter five also discusses the move of DJs into film scoring and explores the synergistic aspect.

10   Popular musicians who have composed music for the occasional film include Adrian Belew, Big Country, Denis Bovell, Ian Broudie, James Brown, Marvin Gaye, Karl Wallinger and Stevie Wonder.

11   This was a collaboration with Laurie Anderson.

12   The *Trainspotting* soundtrack also features Blur's 'Sing' from their first album, *Leisure*.

13   It is unclear how much of the music was written by Albarn and how much was written by Benediktsson or indeed if the two actually collaborated on any of the pieces.

14   In December 2003 Albarn released a limited edition solo album of demos, *Demo Crazy*.

15   In an interview in the *Independent Magazine* Nyman was quoted as saying, 'I don't think I'll ever really become a rock musician, but now I can talk about me and Damon, it gives me a certain amount of street cred.' See Sweet 1999.

16   In an interesting link that brings together some of his side projects Albarn has said that Gorillaz is not really a band anymore, 'We're making a full-length feature film, so the next bit of Gorillaz music will be a film score rather than a pop record' ‹http://www.musicomh.com/interviews/damon-albarn,htm 8 March 2003›.

CHAPTER FIVE

1   Throughout this chapter the term 'independent' is used to identify that area of film-

making outside of the mainstream film industry. It should be noted, however, that Jane Giles uses the term 'underground', which she distinguishes from 'independent' and defines as an alternative to the mainstream (1995: 45).

2 Martin Marks provides a list of these films in 'Music and the Silent Film' in G. Nowell-Smith (ed.) (1996) *The Oxford History of World Cinema*, 186.

3 In contrast to Doty, Smith says *Saturday Night Fever* actually provided the model (1998: 197–8).

4 Smith gives three different definitions of synergy: (i) From Denisoff and Plasketes, 'movie + soundtrack + video = $$$'; (ii) Justin Wyatt 'suggests that synergy is a key component of "high concept" filmmaking insofar as it describes conglomerate activity but also expresses the extent to which almost every aspect of a film is subsumed within the current emphasis on marketing and merchandising'; (iii) Susan Ohmer 'suggests that the term is more appropriate as a description of cross-marketing strategies than as a rubric for present forms of industrial organisation' (1998: 187).

5 Smith notes how in Denisoff & Romanowski's single-minded focus on box-office numbers and chart performance their argument is flawed by a somewhat simplistic economic model – their most significant oversight being their failure to acknowledge the role of scale economies and he discusses this in some detail (1998: 187–9).

6 Smith notes how, after the success of *Flashdance*, MTV became sensitive to charges that it offered free advertising time to Hollywood and thereafter stipulated that future film-inspired videos would have to include the recording artist in at least 50 per cent of the video's footage (1998: 201).

7 This practice of films with hit singles also continued into the 1990s with films such as *Robin Hood: Prince of Thieves* (Kevin Reynolds, 1991), *Four Weddings and a Funeral* (Mike Newell, 1994) and *Men in Black* (Barry Sonnenfeld, 1997), amongst others.

8 Also see Figgis article mentioned in chapter three, note 12.

9 Previous Oscar winners for Best Song have included the following, all from Disney films: 1991: 'Beauty and the Beast' from *Beauty and the Beast*; 1992: 'A Whole New World' from *Aladdin*; 1994: 'Can You Feel the Love Tonight' from *The Lion King*; 1995: 'Colors of the Wind' from *Pocahontas*; 1999: 'You'll be in my Heart' from *Tarzan*.

10 Cave made his film debut in John Hillcoat's *Ghosts ... of the Civil Dead* in 1988, in which he had an acting role as well as contributing dialogue and music. Cave then took on an acting role in Tom Di Cillo's *Johnny Suede* in 1991 and composed the music for Hillcoat's *To Have and to Hold* in 1996.

11 See Barron 2003 and Kermode 1995.

12 In the UK only the original soundtrack was released.

13 Barron notes how this was then followed by *The X Files: the Album* released to tie in

with the film *The X Files: Fight the Future* (Rob Bowman, 1998). This also included some tracks which were included in the film and others that were not. There was also a second album, containing Snow's incidental score for the film, released at the same time.

14 The original soundtrack CD featured Emmylou Harris, Gillian Welch, Alison Krauss and Ralph Stanley; it sold more than 1.5 million copies and was the biggest-selling soundtrack of 2001.

15 There is also a third album, a compilation released by Virgin Records of 'Music Inspired by *Moulin Rouge*'.

16 The 'supergroup' comprised of Greg Dulli of the Afghan Whigs, Dave Pirner of Soul Asylum, Dave Grohl of the Foo Fighters and Thurston Moore of Sonic Youth.

17 This film also uses two 'supergroups', Venus in Furs – which includes ex-Suede member and now solo artist, Bernard Butler – and Thom Yorke of Radiohead. Wylde Ratz includes Thurston Moore and Steve Shelley from Sonic Youth and Ron Asheton from the original Stooges.

GLOSSARY

Definitions given here are related to the specific use made of these terms in their place of appearance in the text.

atonal – music that lacks a tonal centre and tends to have an unsettling effect. (*Tonal* is the term used to describe the organisation of the melodic and harmonic elements to give a feeling of a key centre to the music.)

classical era of music – used to refer to the period from the late 1700s to the mid-1820s, characterised by more rigidly defined musical forms, increased attention to instrumental music and the evolution of the symphony.

classical Hollywood film – used to describe films produced in the Hollywood studio system primarily in the 1930s and 1940s.

classical Hollywood film score – used to describe music in the classical Hollywood film. Largely symphonic, based on musical practices of the nineteenth century, particularly those of romanticism and late-romanticism. Dramatic action would be underscored at every opportunity and the score's formal unity was typically derived from the principle of the leitmotif.

composite – term used to describe a score using a combination of original music, pre-existing classical pieces and pre-existing popular music.

conglomerate – large industrial organisation, usually involved in several different industries.

convergence – the 'coming together' of previously separate industries, which increasingly uses the same or related technology and skilled workers. Convergence is a feature of the contemporary media environment and a product of mergers between companies in different sectors as well as a logical outcome of technological development.

cue – musical segments created specifically for moments in a film.

diegetic music – the 'source' of diegetic music can be observed on screen, for example a character is shown listening to the radio or a CD, music being performed live.

discordant – conflicting notes that often clash or are harsh sounding.

high concept – a 'high concept' film is one that emphasises style and 'stylishness', with a simple, easily summarised narrative. This provides snappy plot descriptions and images to be used as marketing 'hooks'; there is also an emphasis on stars, soundtrack (score and pop songs) and video.

incidental music – short musical segments that accompany or highlight dramatic moments.

independent – used to describe both films and music produced outside of the mainstream entertainment industries.

leitmotif – use of a musical phrase to identify with a particular character or place, or idea.

mickey-mousing – where the music makes the onscreen actions explicit, imitating their rhythm or direction.

modernist – music written in the twentieth century, or contemporary music.

nondiegetic music – music that appears to come from outside the story world, it is often heard as background music and is usually added to the film in post-production.

romantic – the musical period following the classical period, from approximately 1825–1900. Characterised by freer forms, larger, more elaborate works and an increased attention to emotional themes within the music.

spot – identify places on the soundtrack where music would be used.

synergy – the strategy that the common cross-promotion of two or more related products, for example, films and soundtracks, could benefit both industries in almost equal measure. Also used to describe companies attempting to control both hardware and software markets.

temp score – the practice of using music to accompany the film during the early stages of editing, before the score is composed, with various types of recorded music to substitute for the yet to be recorded score.

underscore – musical accompaniment to dialogue.

vertical integration – business activity involving one company acquiring others elsewhere in the production process.

BIBLIOGRAPHY

The bibliography lists works cited in the text and is also designed to point to useful further reading. The list of 'essential reading' highlights works considered to be of particular importance to contemporary understandings of music in film, although many valuable contributions are also to be found under 'secondary reading'.

ESSENTIAL READING

Brown, R. S. (1994) *Overtones and Undertones: Reading Film Music*. Berkeley: University of California Press.

Buhler, J., C. Flinn & D. Neumeyer (eds) (2000) *Music and Cinema*. Hanover: Wesleyan University Press.

Denisoff, R. S. & G. Plasketes (1990) 'Synergy in 1980s Film and Music: Formula for Success or Industry Mythology?', *Film History*, 4, 257–76.

Donnelly, K. J. (1998) 'The classical film score forever? *Batman*, *Batman Returns* and post-classical film music', in S. Neale & M. Smith (eds) *Contemporary Hollywood Cinema*. London: Routledge, 142–55.

_____ (2001a) *Film Music: Critical Approaches*. Edinburgh: Edinburgh University Press.

_____ (2001b) *Pop Music in British Cinema: A Chronicle*. London: BFI.

Doty, A. (1988) 'Music Sells Movies: (Re)New(ed) Conservatism in Film Marketing', *Wide Angle*, 10, 2, 70–9.

Eisler, H. & T. Adorno (1994) *Composing for the Films*. London, Atlantic Highlands, N.J.: The Athlone Press. (Reprint of the Oxford University Press original of 1947 with a new introduction by Graham McCann).

Gorbman, C. (1987) *Unheard Melodies: Narrative Film Music*. London: BFI.

Inglis, I. (ed.) (2003) *Popular Music and Film*. London: Wallflower Press.

Kalinak, K. (1992) *Settling the Score: Music and the Classical Hollywood Film*. Wisconsin: University of Wisconsin Press.

Kassabian, A. (2001) *Hearing Film: Tracking Identifications in Contemporary Hollywood Film Music*. New York and London: Routledge.

Lack, R. (1997) *Twenty Four Frames Under*. London: Quartet Books.

Marks, M. (1997) *Music and the Silent Film: Contexts and Case Studies (1895–1924)*. Oxford: Oxford University Press.

Robertson Wojcik, P. & A. Knight (2001) *Soundtrack Available: Essays on Film and Popular Music*. Durham: Duke University Press.

Romney, J. & A. Wootton (eds) (1995) *Celluloid Jukebox: Popular Music and the Movies since the 50s*. London: BFI.

Smith, J. (1996) 'Unheard Melodies? A Critique of Psychoanalytic Theories of Film Music', in D. Bordwell & N. Carroll (eds) *Post-Theory: Reconstructing Film Studies*. Wisconsin: University of Wisconsin Press, 230–47.

_____ (1998) *The Sounds of Commerce: Marketing Popular Film Music*. New York: Columbia University Press.

SECONDARY READING

Albarn, D. (2001) *Ravenous* DVD commentary.

Allinson, M. (2001) 'Music and Songs', in *A Spanish Labyrinth: The Films of Pedro Almodóvar*. London, New York: I. B. Tauris, 194–205.

Altman, R., McGraw J. & S. Tatroe (2000) 'Inventing the cinema soundtrack: Hollywood multi-plane sound system', in J. Buhler, C. Flinn & D. Neumeyer (eds) (2000) *Music and Cinema*. Hanover: Wesleyan University Press, 339–59.

_____ (2001) 'Cinema and Popular Song: The Lost Tradition', in P. Robertson Wojcik & A. Knight (eds) *Soundtrack Available: Essays on Film and Popular Music*. Durham: Duke University Press, 19–30.

Anderson, L. (2003) 'Case Study 1: *Sliding Doors* and *Topless Women Talk About Their Lives*', in I. Inglis (ed.) *Popular Music and Film*. London: Wallflower Press, 155–77.

Anderson, P. T. (1999) *Magnolia* CD liner notes.

Andrew, G. (1999) Jim Jarmusch NFT Interview – 15 November 1999. On-line. Available: http://www.film.guardian.co.uk/Guardian_NFT/interview/0,4479,110605,00.html. (4 January 2003)

Anon. (2000) 'Aimee Mann Bloom', On-line. Available http://www.ptanderson.com/featurefilms/magnolia/articlesandinterviews/mannmtv.html (24 May).

_____ (2003) On-line. Available http://www.ammi.org/calendar/ProgramNotes/ProgNotesDenisNenette.html (21 February).

Arroyo, J. (1992) 'La Ley Del Deseo: A Gay Seduction', in R. Dyer & G. Vincendeau (eds) *Popular European Cinema*. London: Routledge, 31–45.

Barron, L. (2003) 'Music Inspired By…: The Curious Case of the Missing Soundtrack', in I. Inglis (ed.) *Popular Music and Film*. London: Wallflower Press, 203–23.

Bazelon, I. (1975) *Knowing The Score*. New York: Van Nostrand Reinhold Company.

Beaumont, M. (2003) 'The Thoughts of Chairman Albarn' in *NME*, 17th May 2003.

Bessman, J. (1999) 'Mann Blossoms on Reprise Soundtrack', in *Billboard*, 13 November 1999. On-line. Available: http://www.ptanderson.com/featurefilms/magnolia/articlesandinterviews/magnoliasoundtrackbillboard.html (24 May 2002).

Borrelli, C. (2000) 'Camera! Music! Action!', in *The Toledo Blade*, 6 August 2000. On-line. Available: http://www.ptanderson.com/featurefilms/magnolia/articlesandinterviews/toledoblade.html (24 May 2002).

Brown, Royal S. (1996) 'Modern Film Music', in G. Nowell-Smith (ed.) *The Oxford History of World Cinema*. Oxford: Oxford University Press, 558–66.

Butler, D. (2002) *Jazz Noir: Listening to Music from Phantom Lady to The Last Seduction*. Westport: Greenwood Press.

Carey, M. & M. Hannan (2003) 'Case Study 2: *The Big Chill*', in I. Inglis (ed.) *Popular Music and Film*. London: Wallflower Press, 247–70.

Carroll, N. (1982) 'The Future of Allusion' in *October 20*, Spring, 51–81.

Creekmur, C. K. (2001) 'Picturizing American Cinema: Hindi Film Songs and the Last Days of Genre', in P. Robertson Wojcik & A. Knight (eds) *Soundtrack Available: Essays on Film and Popular Music*. Durham: Duke University Press, 375–406.

Daubney, K. (2000) *Max Steiner's Now, Voyager: A Film Score Guide*. Westport: Greenwood Press.

Denisoff, R. S. & W. D. Romanowski (1991) *Risky Business: Rock in Film*. New Brunswick: Transaction Books.

Dickinson, K. (ed.) (2003) *Movie Music, the Film Reader*. London: Routledge.

Duncan, C. (1995) '*La Haine* Case Study' *Screen International*, 1036, December.

Ehrenstein, D. & B. Reed. (1982) *Rock on Film*. New York: Delilah Books.

Elfman, D. (2000) *Edward Scissorhands* DVD commentary.

Evans, M. (1975) *Soundtrack: The Music of the Movies*. New York: Hopkinson and Blake.

Flinn, C. (1992) *Strains of Utopia: Gender, Nostalgia, and Hollywood Film Music*. Princeton: Princeton University Press.

_____ (1994) 'Music and the melodramatic past of New German Cinema' in *Melodrama: stage picture screen*. London: BFI, 106–18.

_____ (2000) 'Strategies of Remembrance: Music and History in the New German Cinema', in J. Buhler, C. Flinn, & D. Neumeyer (eds) *Music and Cinema*. Hanover: Wesleyan University Press, 118–41.

Flynn, P. (2000) 'Reykjavik 101', *Dazed and Confused*, May.

French, P. (2001) 'From the sound of silents to Hollywood's golden composers', *Observer*, 12 August.

Friedman, L. S. (1999) *The Cinema of Martin Scorsese*. Oxford: Roundhouse Publishing.

Gabbard, K. (1996) *Jammin' at the Margins: Jazz and the American Cinema*. Chicago: University of Chicago Press.

Gallo, P. (1997) 'Keeping score: new ways in film music' in *Variety*, 3 November. On-line. Available: http://www.findarticles.com/cf_iview/m1312/n13_v368/20227143/print.jhtml

Gassen, T. (1995) Music – John Cale Interview in *Tucson Weekly*, 12, 10, May 18–24. On-line. Available: http://www.tucsonweekly.com/tw/05-18-95/music.html (22 February 2003).

Gdula, S. (1999) 'A Different Tune: Greg Araki in all his *Splendor*', *CMJ New Music Monthly*, November.

Giles, J. (1995) 'As above, so below: 30 years of underground cinema and pop music', in J. Romney & A. Wootton (eds) *Celluloid Jukebox: Popular Music and the Movies since the 50s*. London: BFI, 44–51.

Gomery, D. (1998) 'Hollywood corporate business practice and periodizing contemporary film history', in S. Neale & M. Smith (eds) *Contemporary Hollywood Cinema*. London: Routledge, 47–57.

Grant, K. (1999) Damon Albarn Interview in *Toronto Sun*, 6 April. On-line. Available: http://www.canoe.ca/JamMusicArtistsB/blur_qanda.html (8 March 2003)/

Hanson, S. & P. King Hanson (1986) 'Picture Discs', *Stills*, 26, April, 28–30.

Hillman, R. (1995) 'Narrative in film, the novel and music: Fassbinder's *The Marriage of Maria Braun*', in L. Devereaux & R. Hillman (eds) *Fields of Vision: Essays in Film Studies, Visual Anthropology and Photography*. Berkeley: University of California Press, 181–95.

_____ (2001) 'Fassbinder, and Fassbinder/Peer Raben'. On-line. Available: http://www.latrobe.edu.au/screeningthepast/firstrelease;fr0301/rhfr12a (6 July 2003).

Houlihan, M. (2000) 'Magnolia Marks Mann's Return' in *The Chicago Sunday Times*, 7 January. On-line. Available: http://www.ptanderson.com/featurefilms/magnolia/articlesandinterviews/mannchicagosuntimes.html (24 May 2002).

Jameson, F. (1985) 'Postmodernism and Consumer Society' in H. Foster (ed.) *Postmodern Culture*. London: Pluto Press.

Jenkins, H. (1992) *Textual Poachers: Television Fans and Participatory Culture*. New York and London: Routledge.

Karlin, F. & R. Wright (1990) *On The Track: A Guide to Contemporary Film Scoring*. New York: Schirmer Books.

Kassabian, A. (2003) 'The Sound of a New Film Form', in I. Inglis (ed.) *Popular Music and Film*. London: Wallflower Press, 140–54.

Kermode, M. (1995) 'Twisting the Knife', in J. Romney & A. Wootton (eds) *Celluloid Jukebox:*

Popular Music and the Movies since the 50s. London: BFI, 8–19.

Klein, J. (2000) Jim Jarmusch Interview. On-line. Available:http://www.theavclub.com/avclub3609/avfeature_3609.html (24 May 2003).

Knobloch, S. (1997) '*The Graduate* as Rock 'N' Roll Film', *Spectator*, 17, 2, 61–73.

Kubernik H. & J. Pierce (1975) 'Cohen's New Skin', *Melody Maker*, 1 March. On-line. Available: http://www.leonardcohenfiles.com/melmak2.html (10 May 2002).

Levinson, J. (1996) 'Film Music and Narrative Agency', in D. Bordwell & N. Carroll (eds) *Post-Theory: Reconstructing Film Studies*. Wisconsin: University of Wisconsin Press, 248–82.

Levitan, C. (2000) 'Mann reflects on Magnolia's Success' in *CD Now*,13 January 2000. On-line. Available: http://www.ptanderson.com/featurefilms/magnolia/articlesand interviews/manncdnow.html (24 May 2002).

London, K. (1936) *Film Music*. London: Faber and Faber.

Long, A. (2000) Review of *Ordinary Decent Criminal* soundtrack in *NME*, 11 March.

McGilligan, P. & M. Rowland (1990) 'Reeling' and Rockin': The role of rock in the movies', *American Film*, 14, 12, September, 28–31.

Maltby, R. (2003) *Hollywood Cinema* (2nd edn.). Oxford: Blackwell.

Manvell, R. & J. Huntley (1957) *The Technique of Film Music*. London: Focal Press. Revised edition 1975.

Marks, M. (1996a) 'Music and the Silent Film', in G. Nowell-Smith (ed.) *The Oxford History of World Cinema*. Oxford: Oxford University Press, 183–92.

_____ (1996b) 'The Sound of Music', in G. Nowell-Smith (ed.) *The Oxford History of World Cinema*. Oxford: Oxford University Press, 248–59.

Martin, R. (2002a) 'Line Items for a Song', *Filmmaker*, 10, 3, 35–40, 67–69, 71–2.

_____ (2002b) 'How and When To Score', *Filmmaker*, 10, 4, 35–40.

Morse, S. (1999) 'Aimee Mann's Voice Carried Magnolia', *Boston Globe*, 7 December. On-line. Available HTTP: http://www.ptanderson.com/featurefilms/magnolia/articlesandinterviews/mannbostonglobe.html (24 May 2002).

Mundy, J. (1999) *Popular Music on Screen: From the Hollywood Musical to Music Video*. Manchester: Manchester University Press.

Neiiendam, J. (2000) Damon Albarn interview, *Screen International*, 14 July, 21.

Nowell-Smith, G. (1987) 'Minnelli and Melodrama', in C. Gledhill (ed.) *Home is Where the Heart Is: Studies in Melodrama and the Woman's Film*. London: BFI.

Occhiogrosso, P. (1984) 'The beat goes on in a new spate of films with rock tracks...', *American Film*, 9, 6, April, 44–50.

O'Connor D. (2003) Damon Albarn Interview. On-line. Available:http://www.muse.ie/210100/interview/damon.html.

Powrie, P. (2003) 'The Sting In The Tale', in I. Inglis (ed.) *Popular Music and Film*. London Wallflower Press, 60–92.

Prendergast, R. M. (1992) *Film Music a Neglected Art* (2nd edn.). New York: W.W. Norton.

Roberts, C. (2000) 'Sex and Death' *Uncut*, June.

Robinson, P. (2002) Review of *Spider-Man*, *NME*, 11 May.

Roddick, N. (1996) 'A British success: Making and Selling *Trainspotting* Internationally' in *BFI Sight and Sound Supplement*, 10–11.

Ross, B. (2002) The Green Room interview with Stewart Copeland, *southbank*, July and August.

Sergi, G. (1998) 'A cry in the dark: the role of post-classical film sound', in S. Neale & M. Smith (eds) *Contemporary Hollywood Cinema*, London: Routledge, 156–65.

Shumway, D. R. (1999) 'Rock'n' Roll Sound Tracks and the Production of Nostalgia', *Cinema Journal*, 38, 2, Winter, 36–51.

Sinker, M. (1995) 'Music as Film' in J. Romney & A. Wootton (eds) *Celluloid Jukebox: Popular Music and the Movies since the 50s*. London: BFI, 106–17.

Smith, G. (1990) 'Martin Scorsese Interview', *Film Comment*, September/October, 25–30, 69.

Smith, J. (2001) 'Popular Songs and Comic Allusion', in P. Robertson Wojcik & A. Knight *Soundtrack Available: Essays on Film and Popular Music*. Durham: Duke University Press, 407–30.

____ (2001) 'Taking Music Supervisors Seriously' in P. Brophy (ed.) *Cinesonic: Experiencing the Soundtrack*. North Ryde: Australian Film Television and Radio School, 125–46.

Stillwell, R. (1997) 'Symbol, narrative and the musics of *Truly, Madly, Deeply*', *Screen*, 38, 1, Spring, 60–75.

Sweet, M. (1999) 'Orchestral Manoeuvres', *The Independent Magazine*, 28 August.

Thompson, B. (1995) 'Pop and film: the charisma crossover', in J. Romney & A. Wootton (eds) *Celluloid Jukebox: Popular Music and the Movies since the 50s*, London: BFI, 32–41.

Thompson, D. & I. Christie (eds) (1996) *Scorsese on Scorsese* (2nd edn.). London: Faber and Faber.

Tobias, S. (2000) Cameron Crowe Interview. On-line. Available: http:// www.theonionav club.com/avclub3632/avfeature_3632.html (13 July 2003).

Toop, D. (1995) 'Rock musicians and film soundtracks', in J. Romney & A. Wootton (eds) *Celluloid Jukebox: Popular Music and the Movies since the 50s*, London: BFI, 72–81.

Willman, C. (2000) 'Mann Crazy' in *Entertainment Weekly*, 520, 7 January.

Wilonsky, R. (1999) 'Oh Mann' in *Dallas Observer*, 25 November 1999. On-line. Available http://www.ptanderson.com/featurefilms/magnolia/articlesandinterviews/manndallas observer.html (24 May 2002).

Wyatt, J. (1994) *High Concept: Movies and Marketing in Hollywood*. Austin: University of Texas Press.

INDEX OF NAMES